Getting Real

Getting Real

LEE LOZOWICK

HOHM PRESS
Prescott, Arizona

Cover design: Zachary Parker
Cover art: Damentalvaporz crew, Paris, France
Book layout: Becky Fulker

Library of Congress Cataloging in Publications Data

(Application submitted)

ISBN-10: 1-890772-76-3
ISBN-13: 978-1-890772-76-5

Hohm Press
P.O. Box 2501
Prescott, AZ 86302
800-381-2700
www.hohmpress.com

07 08 09 10 11 5 4 3 2 1

For Yogi Ramsuratkumar,
the Source of it all,
and for all the devotees
who have worked so hard,
sacrificed so much
and peeked into the
Vast Reality of the Path.

lee lozowick
Prescott, AZ
3/30/07

Contents

Foreword

As I do less and less formal—read linear—teaching, the events that do happen seem to be that much more potent. After thirty-two years and probably twenty-five thousand hours of talk, talk and more talk, there still seems to be something to say, at least now and then.

In the spring of 2006 we found ourselves (myself and a few students, Lord knowing I certainly would not use the royal "we," not being Pope of anything except perhaps my own neurotic Vatican) in Mexico City for a four-day seminar and food fest of proportions and excellence that would have had to be experienced to be believed (or as my kids say about what they call "situation jokes"—"Ya had to be there."). The following edited (highly: *quelle domage*, we removed the obscenities, most of them, the sales pitches, most of them, and the intolerably long pauses, most of them) talks are both powerful and elevating, intense and revealing, eloquent and—dare I say it? (yes, I dare, tongue-in-cheek, please note)—enlightening, and, believe me, or not, those are some very cool combinations, perhaps equaled only by BLTs, Reubens and Mick and Bianca (that dates me!).

Sadhana, "practice" as we say in English, is not as simple as it may seem upon first blush (kind of like love affairs).

It's like, first things first. Meaning that before we can sail the ocean of bliss, charting those uncharted waters of the Universe, cavorting with God, or at least with the Heavenly Host, or Hostesses, as is both appropriate and Divinely Lawful, we must lay a base, a foundation, that is not only strong and resilient but, perhaps even more important, reliable. In order to build, or lay, as I said before, such a base (construct may apply also), we must realize, or recognize, what obstacles stand in the way, so we don't build (lay, construct, erect) this base on quicksand, a major fault line, shifting sands, or a sacred burial mound. And if you are like me, armored, defended and firmly in denial, this may take some effort and some time.

In any event, the essays that follow are designed, though not intentionally, to serve you in that regard, to help open the "doors of perception" and the windows of refusal to let a little sunlight and fresh air in. And they are meant (though not intentionally) to be entertaining and enjoyable as well. So, if you find yourself—before, during or after reading some or all of this dreck—feeling angry, frustrated, depressed, sad, irritated, elated, euphoric, aggressive, offended, outraged, imbalanced or inharmonious, sentimental, romantic or violent, you've missed the point. How to prepare for what is to come? Relax.

And being the motor-mouth, or diarrhea-hand, that I am, I will buckle down, discipline my self, and stop here.

The Author, somewhat.
March 5th, 2007
Prescott, Arizona
in an uncomfortable chair
behind a massively
crowded and seemingly,
or ostensibly, disorganized
desk.

Introduction

Wake up! Pay attention! The visionary's voice, sounding dimly through the fog of our confusion, is often perceived as jarring or raucous. It speaks to us through many different ways and means as a call to transformation that just won't go away. For the spiritual practitioner, the teacher's shout is an urgent summons to higher conscience: there is no time to fool around. No more time for self-justification and lies; no more time for indulgence in ego's dreams of grandeur, power and control.

The author of this book—who is known for making mischief, as are all gremlins—has never been swayed by popular opinion. However, Lee Lozowick is no mythical person; he is a truly human being who is the spiritual son of the revered south Indian saint, Yogi Ramsuratkumar, and a traditional guru who has been teaching in the West for over thirty years. His message has been and remains centered around the necessity for tradition, practice and the spiritual guide or guru on the Path. The urgency with which he has attempted to reach us over the years—through books, music, poetry, art and an ongoing flow of teachings that are vitally relevant to our times—has continued to expand as we find ourselves at the brink of an apocalyptic era.

We are journeying in a psychedelic wilderness of supersonic, speed-of-light, high-tech sounds and images that flicker in rapid, hypnotic flashes across the screens of our minds; we are drifting on the currents of worldly concerns, while the sound of the teacher's clear voice calls us back to sanity and true selfhood, which exists only in the embrace of the Divine. The world desperately needs those who are loyal to the cosmic law of the self and so are compelled by the integrity of a bigger vision, not only in the compassion and clarity of the teacher, but also the insight and heart of the disciple.

This collection of essays is aimed, without question, at every one who is interested in serious work on self as a student, disciple or devotee in relationship to a teacher, whether that teacher is a guru, roshi, tulku or shaykh. But these are decadent times, in which we find the contemporary Western spiritual scene—whose ostensible purpose is to awaken us and inspire our vision—as deeply quagmired in confusion and ignorance as any other sector of modern life. Particularly in America, California-style neo-advaita—a dissipated reformulation of classic Indian Advaita Vedanta and Hinayana Buddhism—has infected masses of spiritual seekers who are lured by the promise of a quick-fix "enlightenment" that releases us from personal suffering and personal responsibility. Even when well-intentioned, such a promise is ultimately quixotic and dangerous precisely because we can convince ourselves that we are on the spiritual Path, when in fact we are heading in the wrong direction—the direction of self-centered, narcissistic self-aggrandizement and insensitivity to the suffering of others.

Many of us have rejected the poisonous "gifts" of our disposable techno-culture in tangible ways: perhaps we can walk away from the gorgons and sirens of fast food that is devoid of nutrition, or cell phones and Internet relationships that rob us of soul and spiritual substance. But the American psyche is still the product of its cultural milieu, and we are easily seduced by the lure of drive-by spirituality and wholesale enlightenment. The spiritual chimera of personal freedom through enlightenment has become popular merchandize in the consumer marketplace, but while we loll about in beguiling fantasies, the precious jewel of Surrender to Divine Will escapes us entirely.

Another illusion of the contemporary spiritual scene is the proliferation of false teachers—one who has assumed the role of teacher without the breadth and depth of realization and skillful means (to use a Buddhist term) to steer clear of the inevitable seductions of leading others through the rugged and subtle terrain of spiritual transformation. The great majority of these individuals are teaching outside the grace of a true lineage; they pattern themselves as free-spirits with a unique discovery that is for sale and requires no real effort of sadhana or ongoing responsibility on the part of the seeker.

In this book, Lee Lozowick is foremost shouting at, whispering and speaking directly to those of us who have already found a true path and a true teacher. We are the ones who are most profoundly in a position to be responsible. Responsible for what? The consciousness on this planet, to begin with. The generative and graceful function of prayer and the healing and harmonizing forces of faith, clarity, forgiveness, gratitude, praise and a sense of higher purpose. Maybe we can even be responsible for the recognition and cultivation of the Sacred in a soulless and godless society. In order to be responsible, however, we have to get real about where we are really living. What is our internal reality about?

For the great majority of practitioners, ten, twenty or thirty years into the Path and the process of radical transformation, the teacher is still shouting to be heard through the density of the veils that continue to obscure our vision. We have to face the fact that our mechanical, habitual personalities—

motivated by psychological strategies—are still in control of our daily actions. We must find a way to carry on, to renew and regenerate our practice, commitment and faith—for it takes a long, long time, it seems, to purify and alchemize; to ruthlessly contend with the veils that obscure our vision.

During a visit with Lee in 2007, Sufi teacher Llewellyn Vaughan-Lee spoke of 70,000 veils of darkness and 70,000 veils of light that must be penetrated on the spiritual Path. These veils were created by the Supreme Being and are lawful, objective obstacles; in the process of penetrating those veils, we are initiated into greater mysteries. According to Llewellyn, there is another veil or obscuration that exists during our current era, which has been created by humanity; it is the by-product of the once-natural psyche, now twisted and toxified by the poisons of contemporary Western culture. At this point in time, this veil covers the entire Earth; our minds are obscured to our own divine nature, leaving the soul lost and wandering in a wasteland. The human body—with its great potential for revelatory wisdom—is rendered into an empty husk of debilitating emotional storms, addictions and fear.

The only recourse is to find and embrace the sanctuary of the Path and the teacher—the guru. Finding this sanctuary is not the end of the road; on the contrary, the first blush of profound insight, which Lee speaks of in his last essay as the moment of "darshan" or "seeing," is only the beginning of a long journey. When we have our first opening—seeing the oneness of all life, the truth, beauty, love and sanctuary of the guru, the dharma and the sangha—we must then continue to purify the poisons of Western culture and begin the arduous process of working through the 70,000 veils of darkness and 70,000 veils of light. Taking refuge on the Path, we are all the more aware of the greed, hopelessness, dread and fear that plagues humanity; it bleeds through to us, seeps into our hearts, runs through our veins, as we are part of the whole and will naturally feel what is experienced in the body of humanity, the body of the Earth, the solar system, galaxy and—expanding the boundaries of our connectedness until it dissolves completely—even in the Divine.

Early on in Lee's teaching work he described the cycles we move through as we slowly become resonant and aligned with the Great Process of Divine Evolution: Infatuation—Indifference—Doubt, which matures into Insight—Frustration—Remorse at the level of basic human maturity, and Free Moment—Disposition of Enlightenment—Compassion at the level of the heart. These cycles are experienced at every level of the practitioner's journey into awakening, becoming cycles within greater cycles, recurring patterns within patterns as we spiral through the landscape of an ongoing spiritual practice. In fact, these cycles may be understood as another way of speaking about the 70,000 veils of light and 70,000 veils of darkness. Obviously, to navigate such a labyrinth, we need all the help, the reminders, the instruction and transmission that the teacher has to give us.

Clearly, radical transformation is not a quick, facile or ego-gratifying process. It requires supreme effort, courage, conviction and endurance; most of all, it requires a great heart—that is, a heart that may be expanded, through a fiery process, to encompass and embrace the Universe. It is the work of an entire lifetime, and it is this work that ensures we will continue to work in whatever realm or realms we will inhabit beyond the death of our current human bodies. There is no other work to do. As Lee said in his first book, *Spiritual Slavery*, "The work I have come here to do is the same work you have come here to do. I have assumed it, you have not."

---

1 *Living God Blues*, p. 38, Hohm Press, Prescott, Arizona, 1984.

This potent little book titled *Getting Real* consists of a series of teachings that were edited and synthesized into ten essays, originally taken from Lee's discourses at his five-day seminar in Mexico City in May, 2006. Lee's hosts had titled the seminar, "Dinero y Prosperidad" or "Money and Prosperity: How to get it, how to conserve it and how to use it wisely." As usual, Lee touched on the seminar "theme" he had been given, and then he spiraled out to address broader dimensions of dharma, relationship with a teacher and the Path. The result is a configuration of essays that cover a spectrum—from the core realization of nonduality to what Lee calls "Enlightened Duality," from the practical application of the teaching in daily life to transcendent insights of darshan and Surrender to the Will of God.

The title, *Getting Real,* was given by Lee himself, and at least at one level, it seems that Lee is revealing himself in his stark refusal to pander to our need to project a lovely "spiritual master" image on him that fits with our ideas of how things should be. Instead of sitting on a throne of remote spiritual empowerment, in using himself as the example, Lee opens the door for us to "get real" with ourselves. If we have understood the dharma, the teaching and the nature of the guru, we will instinctively and deeply understand that this is a great sacrifice that Lee makes for us. Entrenched in sticky societal influences and bombarded by negative impressions, how can we find a true resonance with the eternal principles of the Path? Lee's skillful and sly debunking of enlightenment and ruthlessly demystifying the role of guru makes the awakened condition uniquely available to us; while the higher context is always present, vulnerability flows naturally. Such a vulnerability and selfless self-revealing is a great example to us—we can only hope to be so real.

Amidst Lee's ongoing declarations that he is not making the teaching communication in a "linear" form anymore (a theme that he reflects upon in the autobiographical mode of the first essay), the dharma continues to flow from him in the spoken word. He says that he is not impelled to "produce information anymore," and yet, it is the experience of many of his friends and students that the nonlinear *transmission* of the teaching continues to come through him—as it has for over thirty years—in the extremely useful and practical linear teachings he gives, when he offers pith instruction and specific guidance in how to live in relationship to the guru and the Path in today's world.

We are extremely grateful to have the opportunity to offer these vital teachings for the benefit of all beings. With these spoken words rendered on paper, we cannot hear the frequent laughter of those who attended this seminar; their chuckles and Lee's smiles were an important part of the mood that carried the dharma along throughout this week of teachings. Hopefully, despite the process of necessary editing, the fresh, spontaneous, intimate quality, the tenderness and compassion, the rich sense of humor and irony (found also in Lee's captions for his photos), and the sometimes rambling, insulting, street-savvy style of Lee Lozowick has been kept intact. So, you are invited to read with the eyes of the heart, and maybe you will *see* the guru's face coming through the words themselves.

The Editor
April 1, 2007
Prescott, Arizona

The Teaching Never Changes

Buenos dias! The books I have to show you this morning are called Study Manuals. Having been in the field of spiritual teaching for thirty years, we've generated a tremendous amount of information. There are nine or ten thousand pages of information, data, education and study material in print, which is probably five percent of what is recorded on tape that eventually may be turned into books. So I don't really have a burning inner feeling that I've got to produce information anymore. The Study Manuals alone are three thousand pages of education. These volumes are especially important for me now, because my approach to teaching is changing so quickly and radically that sometimes I worry that people who really should be meeting this Path are going to be left behind.

The essence of the teaching never changes, but over the years the form has changed quite a bit. On the first trip we took to India, we must have walked fifteen to twenty kilometers every day. We would get up in the morning and say, "Where are we going today?" and then we would head out, climb mountains, walk through the streets—walk and walk and walk and walk. Our trips to India aren't anything like that now, but that's just one thing that has changed.

In the beginning of my teaching work a certain group of people came, and many of those people are still here. I was making all kinds of dramatic teaching lessons in the early days. Once I got very angry with somebody—a woman, of course. We were in California eating at a restaurant, and I said to her, "Let's go outside and continue the argument," because people were eating and I didn't want to disturb anyone. Sometimes two people can get into an automatic roll, and we can't stop making suffering for one another. In this instance, words were coming out of our mouths and our tempers were rising, so we went outside. I was carrying a plate of Mexican food that was covered with guacamole and melted cheese, and when we got outside, I smashed the plate in my face! It was such a shock for the person I was arguing with that there was no more argument. There was a moment of clarity, and we were able to resolve everything very rationally and calmly. Don't try this—but it worked once, anyway!

I used to do very dramatic things like that all the time in the early days, until I realized that I could actually hurt myself that way. I never put other people in danger, but sometimes I would do things that were personally dangerous—dangerous to me. Being very self-centered, I decided that my students were important but not that important.

Before this Work started, I used to teach the Silva Method—a metaphysical training that takes four days and you develop all kinds of psychic abilities. After teaching for a few years, I realized that essentially I could teach the essence of the Silva Method in about fifteen minutes. Jose Silva knew that too; this was no news to him, but he also knew that people need a little bit of theater. People need a little bit of matrix to make something very simple look like it's more complicated, because we just can't believe that something simple is really that simple. In this Work, the transmission is made in fifteen minutes, and then the practice—practice to realize and accomplish—takes the rest of your life.

There was a Russian teacher in the early part of the twentieth century named George I. Gurdjieff, whose teachings and practices were called "the Work."[1] There's a phrase in the Work, which is "to make a super-effort." When you make a super-effort, you tap into a certain energy force that ordinarily you can't bring into your active life. In the sports field today that's called "being in the zone." One minute you're running and you can barely breathe, you think you're going to drop any second, and the next minute you're just sailing along and you could run for days. I had that happen once. "Ah, I can run for days! But where am I going to run to?" And then I thought, "There's nowhere to run to, so why even start running to begin with?"

Years later, one of the things that I began to realize about this Work was that I didn't have to get all dramatic and intrude myself in shocking ways into people's lives in order to make teaching points. All people had to do was live and pay attention, and they'd get exactly the same teaching points. My teaching work moved from feeling that I had to set up circumstances and create a certain kind of drama in order to make a point, to simply encouraging people to pay attention to themselves.

So the teaching changed. Instead of leaning on people—putting them in stressful circumstances to force a discovery of super-effort—I realized that my students would make super-efforts without me standing behind them with a whip. If people wanted something badly enough, they would make super-efforts when necessary.

---

1 Lee uses the Gurdjieffian term "the Work" interchangeably with the more universal term "the Path" to refer to the ongoing process of sadhana, or transformational work on self, within the shelter of a traditional *sampradaya* (spiritual clan or school) and *parampara* (lineage).

Still, I'm kind of an intellectual character, lost in my mind, completely disassociated from my body—except when I'm hungry! In 1976, in the beginning of the community, the ideas were incredibly inspiring. I was just on fire with the teaching. We would start a meeting at seven or eight or nine o'clock at night, and we would keep going until one or two or three in the morning. It was never tiring and never boring. The incredible clarity of the teaching was just a nonstop flow.

I think the average age in the community at that time was twenty-one, so everybody was up for getting no sleep. People had jobs, they had to get up at five or six in the morning, and that's just what we did, week after week after week, month after month. They didn't have children yet, so nobody had to worry about being home for their kids. We generated this fantastic dharma fest.

After a couple of years of that, all the basics were more than well covered. Then we started covering specifics in people's lives: their concerns about their professional life and their relationships. People got into relationships and started having children, which required a different kind of time and energy, and so there was less conversation. We all got busy. Some people opened their own businesses, which required tremendous amounts of effort and time. The flow of information became a little more personal—instead of the universal dharma, it became more about specific issues people were dealing with in their lives.

In the beginning of the community there were about a hundred people, and then it went down to about fifty, then twenty, and eventually, when we moved from New Jersey to Arizona, it was down to about twelve. Slowly, slowly, we built the numbers up. The twelve people who moved to the Arizona ashram had been hearing me speak for five years, and they had more information than they could ever use.

We were still having conversations, but they had a different quality to them. Predominantly I was commenting on other people's work; I would read from Gurdjieff or E.J. Gold or Chögyam Trungpa Rinpoche or some of the more traditional Eastern teachings and just make commentary. I still enjoyed studying myself, so any time I came across anything inspiring, I would share it with the group.

One day I was reading a book on magic by E.J. Gold. I had checked off about two hundred out of four hundred pages that I felt were worthy of commentary to the group. I thought, "This is going to take three or four years to comment on—forget it." I closed the book and that phase changed. I continued to make commentaries on other teachings, but much less than I had before. After that, the amount of time spent in actually discussing the dharma was down to a few hours a week.

In the late 1980s I went to Europe, where I had some conversations with the people who were hosting me. I visited with my students in Germany several times, then Gilles Farcet wrote his book on Western spiritual masters and brought me to France. I wanted to introduce people to my work slowly, so I decided to take a seminar approach—instead of the "here comes the great guru, bow down at his feet and give him all your money" kind of approach, which might have been a *little* too sharp!

Depending upon whether the seminar was two, three or five days long, there were anywhere from four to eight hours of conversation a day. I was back to talking about the dharma again, and after a couple of years in Europe, word was getting back to the American sangha: "You've never heard anything like this before!" The twelve people who originally came to Arizona had heard this kind of teaching flow from me before, but nobody else had. The American sangha started coming to Europe and saying, "Oh my God, you're never like this in America. All you do is sit around and look bored and do crossword puzzles." During the summers I was giving seven, eight or nine seminars, and everything was taped. That's a lot of information.

Every year for nine or ten years I had been going to Europe and actively teaching, then my master died. I had no expectation that there would be any dramatic changes in my teaching style. I just figured things would go on and His Influence would continue to permeate the flow of the teaching. I used to be excited about teaching when I went to Europe. I couldn't wait to get to Europe every year for many reasons. Europeans, like Mexicans, are very different than Americans, one of the differences being that they're warmer. Americans are very cold. Everybody is egotistical, but Americans are so narcissistic that it really expresses itself on a whole different level. In Arizona, I talked a few times a week for an hour or two, but in Europe I was talking thirty or forty hours a week, and everyone was saying that the teaching was absolutely stunning, even sublime. I was excited about getting to Europe because I was enthusiastic about reinitiating this flow of teaching.

One year not long after my master died, when I got to Europe I found myself thinking, "What am I going to say all summer?" That question didn't come up at Hauteville, because I have always been enthusiastic about teaching there, but at the other seminars where I would teach seven or eight hours a day, I found myself thinking, "What am I going to say? I have nothing to say! What am I going to say?" This was especially because in Europe most people's questions were so . . . immature, I think is the word . . . on the level of psychology, as if there was no such thing as a spiritual Path and a practice. I had enjoyed that dynamic before, because it gave me a chance to play—and every once in awhile there would be a great question, and that was interesting too.

So, I found that I wasn't looking forward to giving the seminars, and I thought, "Uh-oh! Something is changing." I gave the seminars the same as always, and they were just as good as always, because I'm a good machine. When the pesos go in the machine, out comes the soda can! But I didn't have the same kind of inner enthusiasm, like, "I can't wait to tear into the teaching."

At the same time that I found myself not having the same enthusiasm for seminars, the Sacred Bazaar was becoming more and more active. The first time we had a Sacred Bazaar there were a few books and a few little pieces on the table that were not very artistic or particularly fine. Then I started to find more sources and more beautiful and rare objects. I started to fall in love with the pieces. The relationship with sacred artifacts is different than relationships with people: of course your artifacts talk back, but in a very different form—and never emotionally. Isn't that great?

So, slowly my whole inner relationship to seminars began to shift, and I began to represent the tremendous wealth of study materials that we've put out over the years—the Study Manuals, for example—as a body of work that could help people at least build a certain foundation upon which they could appreciate more subtle teachings or less linear teachings. I found myself literally wanting to teach in a whole different way: to minimize the approach of linearly answering questions and speaking about the dharma, and to maximize the approach of the nonlinear confrontation of presence and the flow of blessings.

It was very clear to me—clear with absolute certainty—that the gift of the Sacred Bazaar and the transition of my teaching work was the continuing guidance of Yogi Ramsuratkumar. Even though He had left His physical body, this was His guidance. If I'm good, then every shift in the manifestation of my teaching work is a progressive shift, not a digressive shift. Of course, any shift at all disturbs people and creates ripples in the community, because we like things to be predictable and known. We get used to a certain form, and when the form changes we don't like it. But, just as the students get attached to the teacher, the teacher gets attached to the students. When people leave, they're heartbroken, and so is the teacher. I mean real students, not peripheral hangers-on. When peripheral hangers-on leave, so what?

There are always a few peripheral hangers-on—there have to be. There are times in which the peripheral hangers-on are the workhorses of the entire community. While the senior students are sitting around dealing with heavy matters of the spirit, somebody's got to do the work! For us in Arizona, it's, "Thank God for the Europeans and Mexicans," because most of the Americans are too busy dealing with their emotions and psychology to get all the work done. When the Europeans come, we get months of work done in a few days! Not only that, but the Europeans and Mexicans never complain about how much work there is to do! They just throw themselves in enthusiastically and do the work that needs to be done, while the senior students are sitting back "considering."

So, the Sacred Bazaar has become a teaching vehicle, besides being a tremendous gift to everybody. It's difficult for my students, because I'm out at some antique fair, looking around and picking through things, instead of being on the ashram every weekend. There was a very short period of time in Arnaud's teaching work in which he had backed off a little bit from the degree of formal teaching that he was doing at Hauteville, and there was a kind of panic among his students. People were saying, "Oh, Arnaud's not accessible anymore, and I can't talk to him, I can't get to him . . . ." I didn't notice that. I noticed that he was still writing as many letters as he ever wrote and still as available to people as he ever was, except you had to know how to get to him. If you knew how to get to him, he was there. He was never withdrawn; he was never unavailable. You just had to know how to get to him.

I find the same becoming true of me. People are complaining that I'm always traveling. We tour with Shri in Europe for six weeks, and I try to be with the band as much as possible, which means when I'm with the band, I'm not on the ashram. Then Purna and one of his students, who is a phenomenal artist and musician, made a gift to me of my own CD. The shockwaves of that project were so extraordinary that I decided to tour with my own band, the Lee Lozowick Band, *and* with Shri. All the musicians in the Lee Lozowick Band are French, so it's made up of European musicians, and this year is our first tour. It's a two week tour, but I already know that two weeks isn't going to be enough, and next year I'm going to want a longer tour.

So, it's a rough time for some of my students, because there is even more time when I'm away. There are people in the school who are feeling a little bit abandoned; for years I was on the ashram eighty percent of the time, and now I'm on the ashram twenty percent of the time. People don't like that, obviously. There are ways to get access as deeply and profoundly as there ever was—is it "was" or "were"? English is my second language. My first language, unfortunately, is something no one here would understand—at least not with your minds . . .

So, the teaching has not changed, but it is moving in a very different realm, which is one of the reasons I told everyone that I would only come to teach in Mexico every other year instead of every year. When I was first asked to teach in Mexico, I said at the time that I just traveled too much, but really it was because I'm getting tired of giving linear teachings. I love the people here, the culture and everything else—but all this *talking*! But, as you can tell from this morning, I'm a good machine: the flow keeps going.

We were joking around last night that maybe the next time I come we should just eat and go shopping—save the evenings for movies! Still, it really worries me. I don't obsess about it, but it worries me that new people who come around in the future—who really should be here—will find the form of the teaching just too obscure, too provocative, too inaccessible.

In one sense, my job is defined by serving people who need to be connected into the Work. Everybody needs the Work, but most people will never get to it in this lifetime because different people have different potentialities—not ultimately, but immediately. When I see someone with a great potential, and they just can't get through the veil of theater for some reason, it's a little upsetting because I can't do my job with that person. People who *have* to be here will get here no matter what—that always happens. Whatever the fence is, whatever the obstacles, whatever mountains they have to climb, people who *have* to be here *will* get here, no question. And, there are those people who could really benefit from the Work, but their relationship to it is somewhat delicate because of their own minds.

Even more than worrying that people who should be here won't get here, I worry that people who are already here will be so confused and feel so betrayed by the change in the form of the teaching that they will leave. Sooner or later everybody hits a wall. We all have knots within us that sooner or later the Work is going to reveal as we deepen our insight into our own complex. There's a certain level at which, when we hit that wall, the only thing that can help is Benediction—and adherence to practice, of course.

So, it's important to use the literature of the school as an important element of the early first-stage teaching—the basics, so to speak—to immerse ourselves in a matrix of understanding and clarity about the teaching and the guru and who the guru is. On some paths there is no study—you don't read or use your mind, you just work and use your body. I haven't gotten there yet, if I ever will. To me, study is an important element of establishing a certain understanding, a certain openness of mind, a certain generosity of response to the Work.

Yogi Ramsuratkumar didn't read much in the last years of His life. He did read the newspaper every day—the *Hindu Times*—and He was very well aware of the social and political situation in the world. But, He had His attendants read dharma books to Him all day long; He would have books about Ramakrishna, or whatever books intuitively came to him, read to Him. Occasionally He would make recommendations to some of His Indian devotees to study a certain scripture and really work with it, make it a life's work. I don't know if He ever did this for His Western students—I guess He didn't have to with me, because I'm always reading, reading, reading, reading.

I feel that it's useful to involve all three centers, the way they recommend in the Gurdjieff Work to engage the intellectual center, the feeling center, and the moving center. Very loosely speaking, on the outer level of my teaching, I recommend study, exercise, meditation and other practices that involve all three centers at different times and sometimes all at the same time. If you're creating the kind of art that I appreciate, we could say the creation of art—sculpture, painting, writing—involves all three centers at the same time.

Ouspensky, I think, once asked Gurdjieff what the source of the Work was, and he answered "mystic Christianity." The Gurdjieff Work tends to be very practical and immediate and not at all theistic, but the ultimate source of universal Blessing is an element that can be understood in a context of the Work. Somebody asked me once if my Path could be ultimately effective without the principles of the Work involved, and I said no, I don't believe so. Sometimes people will visit our ashram and get a glimpse of things, and they'll say, "Oh, this is a bhakti yoga path," and I say, "Not entirely." Without the Work aspect, this is not a viable Path.

"Bhakti" means love in Sanskrit—devotional love. Certainly there's an element of devotion, because the more you give yourself to something the more you are infused by the thing you're giving yourself to. Of course you want to make sure that if you give yourself to something, you give yourself to the right thing. You do not want to be infused with what you get if you give yourself to heroin.

Often we are looking for something with a sense of adventure, and we're completely naïve and unprepared for the consequences of what it is that we'll find if we actually find the thing we're looking for. So you want to be very careful what you give yourself to. For example, one of the popular things in the American self-development movement today is *ayahuasca* ceremony. It's very different when someone who lives in a culture in which the ayahuasca plant has been used for generations enters into a ceremonial relationship with the spirit of ayahuasca, and when someone who is culturally and intellectually divorced from that culture enters into the ayahuasca ceremony. Although I've never experimented with drugs, I imagine—and I'm always right about such things—that the spirit of ayahuasca is a little bit mischievous, and it doesn't offer the same thing to each person who enters into relationship with it. I think that the spirit of ayahuasca will serve some people and will totally squash other people.

Yogi Ramsuratkumar rarely answered questions; instead, He either laughed or referred to Himself as a "beggar" and a "sinner." He was very intelligent. He spoke fluent English; He was a headmaster of a school when He was working. He knew all the classics of Western literature, which was embarrassing to us because occasionally He would ask us if we could recite Milton or Virgil or Blake, and none of us could.

I remember once He asked me to tell the story of Romeo and Juliet. I knew Shakespeare, although I couldn't quote it, and I told the story wrong—not the whole story, but little details. Ma Devaki, who was Yogi Ramsuratkumar's attendant, and the women who were with me were just chomping at the bit to correct me. Devaki is very highly educated, really a brilliant woman, and she knew that I was telling the details wrong. She wanted to make sure that Yogi Ramsuratkumar got what He was looking for, and that the details were right. It's Romeo and Juliet—what difference do the details make? After the session we were walking home and one of the people in my group whispered, "You had the story a little wrong." Immediately my posture changed, my head went down, my tail went between my legs! "I'm sorry," I whimpered.

So, even though He was highly educated, Yogi Ramsuratkumar didn't give people intellectual answers. Sometimes He would just say, "Oh this beggar is just a stupid beggar. This beggar doesn't know anything." This made highly intellectual people very upset: of course everybody knew that he was highly intelligent and knew plenty. Oh, that would get people angry! Sometimes people, mostly Westerners, would say, "Yes you do, I know you know the answer." He would respond, "No, this beggar is so stupid. Go ask some professor, or go ask some sage. This beggar doesn't know anything." Of course that never bothered me, because I never asked Him any questions.

Yogi Ramsuratkumar taught through transmission, meaning that you would just spend time with Him if you could. I was very lucky and my students were very lucky—we really got to be up close with Him when we went to India. We spent a lot of time with Him and had a lot of intimate glimpses of Him that most people never had, but ultimately we didn't need that. It was wonderful, and we were very lucky to have it, but we didn't need it.

One of my students in Mexico asked me the other day if it would be useful to have more correspondence, more phone calls, more contact. Of course, you can always call or write a letter, but you're left essentially to your own intelligence and maturity. I said, "We have enough contact. More is nice, but there is more than enough contact to get the work done that needs to be done." Transmission requires faith, obedience, attention and intention but not necessarily lots of physical proximity between the transmitter and the transmittee.

If you lived in the fifteenth century and you found your master—which would probably cost you your entire life savings and every material thing you owned and possibly your health—maybe you would work with the master for a week, two weeks, a month or even a year or two, and then you'd be sent away for years. The master would say, "Don't come back until you've realized this certain thing," which might take ten years. You couldn't write a letter and you couldn't make a phone call—you were left to your own intelligence and commitment to the Path. You were left to your inner connection.

Every time we have a little argument with our husbands or wives, or every time one of our children does something that disturbs us, we can't call the teacher and ask, "What should I do?" The teacher is not our husband or wife, or our child or mother or father or boss. If we are realistic with ourselves, we will recognize that in many cases when we get direct, linear input from the teacher, we don't use it anyway. When we ask the teacher a question we often have a very clear idea of the answer we want to hear. In our honor and respect for the teacher, we would like the teacher to confirm what we are already feeling. If the teacher gives us a different answer, in many cases, maybe in most cases, we do what we wanted to do anyway!

I've been teaching now for about thirty years. About twenty-five years into the Path we hit a certain kind of phase, which is: nothing has changed. People have been around for twenty-five years or more, they're still on the Path, they're working hard—and, they still have bad habits. They come to me saying, "I've been doing this for twenty-five years, and nothing has changed. I'm the same person I was twenty-five years ago. What's up about that, Master? Explain this to me. I thought I was going to be enlightened fifteen years ago." So I say something like, "What book ever told you that if you got enlightened, you wouldn't still have bad habits?"

I don't know if all the teachers I hang out with are enlightened or not. The people who I think really have wisdom all have bad habits—or at least one bad habit! We have this vision of enlightenment, but it's never what you think it is. Twenty years later, you still have the same bad habits. We tend to have this view of enlightenment that if we were enlightened we would be healthy, impervious to any kind of external negativity and psychologically sane. Not necessarily. You can't control the world. You can eat well, and you can breathe well and drink good water, but we live in a polluted world. It doesn't matter how well you eat or how pure your life is—you can't necessarily say you're not going to get cancer. You have to breathe and the air is polluted.

Second hand smoke is a big thing in America. I never smoked. I go on tour in Europe with my bands, and a lot of the gigs we do are at big festivals. The stages are outside in the mountains. We did a gig last year in the Swiss Alps where the air is so clean—oh my God, it was so beautiful! My students who used to smoke loved it, and I was saying, "Fuck, man!

Give me a small, dark, smoky club anytime. Fuck the mountains, man!" My favorite gigs are when we're tight, hot, close, crammed in, and there's so much smoke you can't even see the back wall! I love it that way. The reality is that second-hand smoke is healthy compared just to walking downtown in Mexico City!

Arizona is one of the cleanest states in America—it's in the desert, it's pure—but Phoenix is surrounded by hills. It's in what is called "The Valley," where every bit of urban pollution just gathers and sits. Pittsburgh and South Bend, Indiana and Chicago—where they have steel mills—are worse. Second-hand smoke? Forget it. You could live on second-hand smoke twenty-four hours a day and it wouldn't be half as bad as the air in Pittsburg! You think nicotine is bad? Try breathing sulfuric acid for a while, because that's what's in the air from industrial waste. Sulfuric acid is much worse than nicotine, and you are breathing that stuff in. We're worried about second hand smoke? We think we're going to be healthy? Forget it.

Look at it this way: Okay, you aren't enlightened. You aren't transformed. You aren't saving the world. The world is still full of violence and aggression; the air and the water and the earth are all polluted. You can't take care of the world, so just take care of *your* world. In your personal space, surround yourself with beauty of any kind. Do anything you can to surround yourself with beauty, harmonious relationships, sacred space and beautiful art, because that's what we have, and that's where the Sacred Bazaar comes in.

So, the teaching never changes, *and* the outer style of my teaching work is changing very dramatically. One way it is changing is that a lot of the spaces that are more commonly available with me are not linear teaching spaces; they are happening in interactions with the Sacred Bazaar, with the art projects, with one of the bands. You need to be sophisticated enough to figure out how to get the same juice that you feel you're getting when you sit face to face with the teacher and ask a linear question to get linear information.

You want to absorb whatever you can absorb when you're in the immediate presence of the Work—the teacher and the teaching. Then you have to understand that *you* are going to have to make sense of it. Having made sense of it, then you need to apply it in your day to day life. Having absorbed the teaching, you should be able to implement the teaching in ordinary circumstances. You want to draw from the teacher's presence and Influence and allow it to clear away all the debris and garbage, to purify all the toxicity, so that you end up being a clear channel for the Blessing of the Divine. Then you can be a clear representative of the Work.

ॐ

Money

Money is like pussy. I don't know how other people define money in terms of it having masculine or feminine energy, but to me, money has feminine energy, and feminine energy is about relationship. I don't just mean money; I mean all things material—the whole material world—because when I use the word money, it represents the feminine principle, not the masculine principle.

In the Baul tradition, which is my tradition, they say that only men have to practice, because women already *are* everything that men have to work to realize. "Pussy" is the American slang word for the feminine sexual organ, so pussy is considered the doorway, the gateway, to transformation for a man. In the Baul tradition—even in India, one of the most male chauvinist countries in the world, with the exception of the Muslim world—women are actually worshipped as divine. Spiritually they already are what is true, what is real, what is complete and perfect and stainless and unattainable. Women are already that which is Real. Unfortunately, in the three dimensional world, they are as neurotic as you can imagine! So, women don't need to be transformed spiritually, but they do need to become a little bit sane.

They've done research in America on people who have won a lot of money in lotteries and found that people's lives tend to fall apart when someone who doesn't have much money suddenly wins a lot of money or gets a big inheritance. That's because, like pussy, money is expensive. Money has a price. You have to be able to manage it, hold it and use it wisely, or the backlash from managing and using it badly is very severe. Like pussy, if you use money badly, you take your life in your hands.

There is a lawfulness relative to the involvement of our energy in the flow of money that comes to us. Suppose you have a passive income from investments, from a trust fund, from a rich relative, or whatever—lucky you, good karma! The way to respect and honor that gift of the Universe is to use the money in a way that is just, that has integrity—don't gamble it away or drink it away or drug it away or whore it away. You might think it would be difficult to whore money away, but there are some very expensive women out there! It is lawful to use the money in a way that is productive and creative and useful—ideally in a sphere beyond your own personal life.

As I become more and more involved in the Sacred Bazaar and less and less involved in the linear teaching, some people have moved into that transition very easefully and gracefully, and others have had some difficulty with it. The Sacred Bazaar began as a kind of hobby—a little side interest of mine—and it has become the central focus of my entire process. I am very serious about those artifacts, that art. That's where I live.

I said to a few of the people who were hosting us this year in Mexico that I hoped this seminar would be really powerful, but we may have had the best teaching already, because we started to unload the Sacred Bazaar yesterday and the few people that happened to be lucky enough to be there began their interaction with it. You will get something very different from me at the tables of the Sacred Bazaar than you will get from me up here. The Sacred Bazaar is where I live; the seminar is where I work. You know the difference. Giving seminars is my profession; the Sacred Bazaar is my life.

If you are a therapist, you can understand how it is to be working with clients, and then how it is to be at home in your own space, cooking and doing what you love, trying not to relate to your lover in psychological terms, as a therapist to a client. I relate to all of the adults in my life—everyone but my children—as a spiritual master to disciples, and it's not a good thing, but I have no discipline. I assume if you are a therapist that you have some sanity and some discipline, so when you go home you can leave your work at the office.

There are a couple of big factors involved relative to financial success. One is karma. Some people just find themselves in the midst of a circumstance in which money comes easily, and if it goes, more comes easily. Other people seem to struggle and struggle and struggle. When we struggle, if money falls into the same category as our psychological issues, then the vast majority—maybe even ninety percent—of our struggle is unnecessary and self-created. Maybe ten percent of our struggle is life. If you are on the way to the airport, stuck in a traffic jam because of a gigantic accident on the highway, it has nothing to do with your attitude. You know, sometimes life just gets in the way. But if you open a business—whether you have a physical location, or you are an artist trying to sell your art to galleries, or whatever it might be—assuming that you are sensible about your approach, if you are struggling, it is usually because of you.

When you are struggling, a lot of it is about context. There is something to being in the right place at the right time, but there are also key elements in financial success—not just getting money but using it wisely and keeping it. A good friend and student from Europe was just visiting us in Arizona. She has no problem making money and lots of it, but she has a terrible time keeping it; it comes in, but then it just seems to disappear. With the world being what it is, you want to have a little bit of reserve; you never know when you are going to need to be able to go someplace quickly, not just because of human problems but because of natural problems.

The entire state of California is sitting on a major fault line on the crust of the Earth. There have been a few times in which, metaphorically speaking, if I had been a half inch to either side of where I was, I'd be dead now—fallen off a cliff or broken into pieces on the side of some highway or overdosed on drugs. Just a little bit off from where I was, and I would have been dead. Some people do die. They just move a little bit off course, the guardian angel is sleeping for a few minutes, and—the end! The Earth is like that. The crust of the Earth is part of a body. It's holding steady, but one little shift and California is in the ocean along with thirty or forty million people—including hundreds of false spiritual masters, so that wouldn't be so bad! And thousands of therapists, which wouldn't be so bad either! So it's good to have a little reserve, resource-wise, because you never know when you are really going to need something.

Karma is not so much in our hands. There are things you can do about it, but you can't completely eliminate it. You can mute or minimize the effects of it, so instead of losing your life, you just come close to losing your life—that kind of thing. Context is something you *can* do something about. It sounds very easy but it is not, because in order to shift context, you have to change your worldview, which is a very difficult thing to do.

There was a movie made by an American social activist named Michael Moore about 9/11, but the name of the movie came from a science fiction book, *Fahrenheit 451*, which is the temperature that books burst into flame. The book was about the burning of good literature and government domination. In the movie there were two scenes in which Michael Moore was interviewing a woman whose son was a soldier serving in Iraq. She said, "I support my President, I support my country, and my son is fighting for our freedom." Then her son got killed in the war, and Michael Moore interviewed her again, and she was rabidly anti-Bush. "He's killing our children!" She even went to Washington D.C. with an anti-war sign and marched in front of the White House. She is a good example of someone who did not have a change of worldview.

An emotional reaction is not a change of worldview. She was in the midst of a completely emotional, reactive state. She was angry that her son had died, and she wanted revenge on whoever was responsible for his death. That was not an intelligent reaction, unfortunately. It ruined the movie for me, because I thought Michael Moore completely manipulated that circumstance to get a certain emotional reaction from the audience. In the end he didn't get that reaction—he got the opposite reaction from me. So, to change your worldview you have to alter the literal root structure of what creates your intelligence, and you don't do that by changing your belief system. You do that by changing your entire psychological story—your script.

We may have grown up in an environment of tremendous ease and relaxation around money, whether we have it or not—or we may have grown up with nothing but tension, tension, tension around money. I was very lucky; my father had no tension about money. My mother worked and managed their money, and when he needed some, she gave it to him. My father was an artist and money meant absolutely nothing to him. During the American Depression of the 1930s, they lived in the mountains of New York State. They lived by a stream and drank the water and bathed in the stream and basically slept in a tent. They had no problem. My father was totally relaxed about money. It didn't bother him if he didn't have it, and if he had it, he didn't care that much. My father's passions were art and ideas and beauty and truth and justice. Money and things didn't mean anything to him. So I was very lucky because my father was my primary influence, and my context for money is not a context of need and struggle and survival. I'm just lucky, that's the way I grew up. On the other hand, unlike my father, what money can *do*—how it can move things, what it can create and the opportunities it can create for people—is very interesting to me.

I drive a car that's ten years old, and I'll probably be driving it for another fifteen years. It's a good car. I don't need a new car. When money comes my way, I don't use it for myself. I have beautiful things in my environment, but I don't use money for houses and cars and clothes and jewelry. Sometimes I wear a necklace, but that's because it has a sacred significance. I have some tattoos, and all of them are sacred Hindu and Tibetan imagery—and one little piece from ancient Egypt. Just by virtue of its presence in your environment or on your mind or on your body, sacred imagery has an effect, just like the pictures of Yogi Ramsuratkumar, Swami Prajnanpad and Arnaud Desjardins. When there are archetypical symbols on you or in your environment or in your sensory field—in your mind—those things have an influence on your entire consciousness and your physical body as well.

So, my teaching work used to be very linear and common sense, and it has changed dramatically since my Master died. I am still randomly doing seminars, but that's not where I live. I live at the tables of the Sacred Bazaar, in the domain of the paradoxical, the enigmatic, the symbolic, because more and more my teaching work is becoming exactly that. In a few years I can easily see a probability of no seminars—just dinner parties and shopping trips and the entire transmission of the teaching being made through personal transactions and the Sacred Bazaar.

I view money as the energy of possibility. I like movement—movement, movement, movement! Every time somebody buys two, three, four or five pieces, it's movement. That's what feeds me. I don't keep a lot of money. I get it in and move it out in some way. The money that goes through the Sacred Bazaar doesn't go to me. It goes to help the alchemist I know complete his work; it goes to help certain artists, who are students of mine, to have more liberty to create their art. It goes to a variety of different places but not to my children, not to my family, not to my personal life. I don't need it, and that's not the purpose of the whole thing.

One of the laws of successful relationship to money is movement. Like consciousness, like water, like most things in life, when these things stagnate, they start to deteriorate or become poisonous. Money is the same. It's good to have a little bit on the side, just in case. At the same time, if your attitude is one of fear and stagnation relative to money, it will become toxic instead of useful. So, one of the ideas of money is to keep it flowing, keep it flowing. There's more money in the world than any of us could possibly use. Keep it flowing. Always make sure you have enough to pay the rent and buy your children an ice cream cone, but keep it flowing, keep it flowing, keep it flowing.

Purna and I gave a seminar on money in France last summer, and I am not going to duplicate that seminar here. I said to everybody in Europe—and I meant it—that I would never do that seminar again. It was a one-time opportunity. It wasn't videotaped or audiotaped. Who was there was there;

who wasn't, wasn't. But I will cover the essence of what that seminar was about, which is context, context, context.

To get the right context, you have to alter your worldview. If you are going to alter your worldview, it requires literal change at the root structure of your intelligence, not up at the surface of things. The roots are underground. They're buried. You are going to have to dig a little bit. The roots of your intelligence are not like the tiny little roots of cactuses that don't need much water. The roots of your intelligence are like the gigantic roots of oak trees that go all the way down. That's how the psyche is.

I grew up on the East Coast of America where it is green, with lots of big trees. Then we moved to Arizona where they have these gigantic saguaro cactuses, ten, fifteen, twenty meters high—and they have tiny little roots. It was always amazing to me because on the East Coast where I lived, you would try to pull out little weeds and they had such deep roots that you would have to dig all the way down just to get the weeds out. The roots of these cactuses are so tiny that animals can almost push them over.

So our psychological roots are deep, sometimes even from the womb. If your mother worked in a market when she was pregnant with you, and all day long in the market there was loud music—the same beat, all day long—you are psychologically defined by the influence of that music. That's just the way it is. It is well known that the emotions a woman lives through during her pregnancy affects the chemical structure of the child. Our psychological roots go way back; they are very deep, and you *can* shift context. You can change your worldview completely and totally, and it requires effort. Deep effort.

I had no Jewish education whatsoever. I was the only Jewish kid in my entire school until I was a teenager. I was with all kinds of people from all kinds of ethnic and racial backgrounds; I didn't realize that everybody has prejudice against somebody. That was before fundamentalism became so popular in America. As I grew up one of the things I would say to my parents was, "Are we Jewish? Am I Jewish? Tell me the truth." I thought maybe I wasn't Jewish because I didn't go to synagogue all the time. My parents would say, "We are culturally Jewish, not religiously Jewish." That was very helpful—not then, but now—because my worldview is more culturally influenced than socially, politically or religiously influenced, which makes it broader and deeper rather than narrow and pious.

Everybody has a worldview. Some of the elements of it are obvious: your political leaning or your social concern, your religious affiliation. Some of it is very subtle, like people who can't have sex unless the lights are on—or people who can't have sex unless the lights are off. For some people, if the lights are on they are paralyzed, but if the lights are off they're animals. If I was in relationship with somebody in either of those two categories, I wouldn't care about them becoming normal and losing their neurosis. I would either turn the lights on or off, as they wished—who cares, just give me the goods!

Money is useful and powerful. It has its own center, its own momentum, its own force. It resists domination and control the same way that we all resist domination and control. All successful relationships are about a little bit of give and take. You move a little bit towards your partner, they move a little bit towards you, and somewhere or other you meet. There is a lawfulness to human relationship, and there is a lawfulness to money—one of the laws of money being movement. Like water, if you stop the movement of money for too long, it becomes poisonous.

If you are in relationship with money relative to its laws—not your laws but its laws—you'll have a very easy time, and money will respond to you enthusiastically and positively. If you try to manipulate or alter the cosmic lawfulness of money, it will not respond to you positively and it will lock up. It may even become aggressive. Do you know what I mean by money being aggressive? One of the ways money can be aggressive is by creating a circumstance in your life in which you are being demanded to give a lot of money for something that is useless.

This might be the most important thing I say in the entire week: never underestimate the power of your mind to manipulate reality. The mind can create a circumstance in your life that will cost you a lot of money, giving you a lesson for being unlawful in relationship to it. The mind can move mountains, literally. It usually doesn't, but it can.

Levitation, for instance, is considered a miracle. But the only reason it's considered a miracle is because most people don't have the discipline to train their minds to be able to levitate at will. It is a process created by the mind and sustained by the mind. It is a very easy thing to do if you are willing to pay the price of the training, which most people aren't—so, there you are.

In order to develop a healthy relationship to money in which there is no scarcity whatsoever, neither physically nor mentally, you have to train the mind, because the mind controls your worldview. Like radio and television control the impressions that come through them: you can't hear the music if you don't turn the switch. The mind is the switch. Sooner or later you're going to have to work with your minds. The fact that there are historical examples of people who have transcended the grip of their mentalizations in a moment—like Ramana Maharshi, for example—does not make a rule. There are exceptions to the rules. We are not likely to be those exceptions. If we were going to be those exceptions, we would have been already, a long time ago. By the time you've got to dye your hair so you don't see the gray in it, it is highly unlikely you are going to be an exception to the rules!

Ramana Maharshi was sixteen years old when his shift took place. There was a book out years and years ago, in which somebody researched a number of what he called "realized people," not only Jesus and Mohammed but also artists and scientists: Walt Whitman, William Blake and other people. The author of the book said that the average age of this major shift in worldview is in the early thirties, and the likelihood of being an exception to the rule after that becomes less and less the older you get.

However, there are great people, like St. Teresa of Avila, who were not an exception to the rules. She paid her dues. She paid the price, did the work and changed her worldview. If you read her writings, you see that she worked on herself. After her shift she was very human, very real. She had a great sense of humor, and she was a great artist, poet, writer. She was not like Anandamayi Ma, who was transcendental. She was physically beautiful, but she wasn't a woman. Anandamayi Ma wasn't even human; she was in some other category. She is one of the exceptions to the rules, but the fact that there are exceptions to the rules doesn't mean that we should count on being exceptions to the rule. We need to work. Work, work, work, work!

So, you have to deal with your mind. We were sitting at breakfast yesterday, and someone came out with a pitcher of cactus juice. It looked tasty and attractive, then she started to pour it and I saw the consistency of it. It didn't look so good. I thought, "Drinking that stuff is going to be like drinking . . ." Well, never mind! But, you know, everybody was having some and they were saying, "Oh, it's very healthy," so I say okay. I had some, and it wasn't so bad! It was mixed with orange juice so it was palatable. In fact, I even had some this morning also, twice in a row—but this morning it was mixed with pineapple juice, so it was much better.

The first thing my mind did when it saw the consistency of that juice was say, "I'm not touching that stuff!" I don't do things like this anymore—it's just so stupid—but when I was a baby guru, about thirty years ago, I served my students horsemeat. I didn't tell them it was horsemeat, because people don't eat horsemeat in America; horsemeat is for dogs. We added mushrooms and herbs, and we made very tasty hamburgers. After everybody ate it, then we told them it was horsemeat. Their reactions were everything from saying that it was pretty good to one person getting sick. It's all in the mind.

You have to deal with the fact that it's all in your mind, but that does not mean that the muscles and glands aren't impacted by what's in the mind. To some degree the hormones that your glands secrete, especially when there is an imbalance, are defined by your mind and your primal psychology—your worldview. Most men probably have the experience, I certainly do, of being with a woman, and she starts to massage your shoulders and says, "God, you've got to relax!" You growl, "I am relaxed! This is relaxed! You should see me when I'm not relaxed!" That's because our musculature is defined by our worldview.

Sometimes we don't know how tense we are; sometimes the degree of our stress is so well managed that we don't even know we've got stress in the body. It's just the way we live, and it seems natural. Then we go to a certain kind of massage therapist, and they say, "Oh my God, you are completely out of whack." We say, "I feel pretty good, I feel fine." Someone who knows the body can look at us and see what we are holding. That is our worldview. We're always defending, walking around with some part of our body on alert. After years of that, our musculature is wrecked, and of course our glands are completely imbalanced.

One of the things that you have to deal with when you are working for a shift of context is to somehow come to terms with your life *now*—not your life when you were a child or a young person. You are walking around defended, so what are you defending against? Your father or your uncle or your older brother or the priest or whoever. You are defended against somebody that is probably dead by now, who is not in your life and has nothing to do with your life today. You are still walking around all day long in a posture of defense, and the person you're defending against is nowhere near you.

So, money is like pussy. If you understand what money is and its potential, and you respect it and honor it for that, then the world opens up. Pussy is a doorway, and you know what that means: the longer you can keep it open, the more likely the possibility that you'll be able to walk through it fully. The same is true of money. Robert Svoboda, who is a practitioner of a very serious tantric path from India, had an Indian master who said, "We Aghoris can have all the money in the world if we want it. It's just that we don't want it." That is because money, like pussy, has a price. It doesn't come for free. You have to be willing to pay the price.

There are laws of money and laws of love. One of the laws of love has to do with giving and receiving. Obviously, if you don't know how to give or receive money, it won't be your friend. For example, when Mother Theresa was working in Calcutta, she had a lot of Westerners come to work with her as volunteers. There was a wealthy European woman who came to work for some weeks, and she didn't want to get down on her hands and wash the lepers, even though she was touched in her own way. She went out and bought Benetton clothes for two hundred children, then she took them to the orphanage. She wanted to dress the children in the clothes, but Mother Theresa had trained her nuns well; they took the clothing and put it in a warehouse. The wealthy woman was so upset about it that she left. The point is that it's important to know how to give, and when and what.

It's also important to know how to receive. I sometimes go out to dinner with at least nine people; sometimes it's a lot more. We were traveling in California and there were twelve of us for dinner. When it was time to pay, I looked up and saw one of my students signing the bill. He knew I was going to treat everybody, but he just walked up and took the check before it got to me. It wasn't dramatic at all; it was just the way he wanted to treat his teacher. He was very pleased, because it was a gift to him to be able to take care of the dinner party, and in this case, I didn't argue. So, we have to learn how to receive—to be in a flow of reciprocity.

I hate to tell you this, but there are laws of love. I know we like to think that love is spontaneous and free, but love is not spontaneous. All those things we think are spontaneous—sentiment and romance—are all shit, nothing but projections, expectations and illusions. There actually are laws of love. One thing is that time makes a difference. If you spend five years with someone, you build something together, but if you spend twenty-five years with someone, you build something really different. When we've been with someone for a long time, most of the things we think are really problems are not really problems at all. Have you ever been with someone so long that the way they chew their meat drives you crazy? You feel that if they keep chewing their meat that way, you're going to choke them! But then the thought goes away and you think, "Ooo, I'd like them to chew on my . . . . like that!"

When we make the effort to work through difficulties over twenty or thirty years, we realize that it was worth it.

I believe in tradition. I'm not very modern, and maybe it's very old-fashioned, but I don't see a lot of depth in the way the world is these days. Like sex: it's a nice thing, but the Universe doesn't revolve around sex! Did you ever see insects having sex? It looks pretty strange to you, doesn't it? To the Universe, sex between humans is like watching sex between flies! But look at what you are willing to do if you are sexually frustrated. Look at what *people* are willing to do if they are sexually frustrated. Sex is really overrated. It's a nice thing—one of the nicest things in life; it's right up there with chocolate and crème brulee—but when you have no money, do you think about sex? No. So how important can it be? We want to be able to keep a perspective about these things. Love functions according to laws; love is not spontaneous.

When men realize that the woman they are with is a carbon copy of their mother, it's a big shock: "Oh my God! I am married to my mother!" Well, so what? Once you figure that the woman you're with is not really your mother, the sex is going to change—for the better! At least we hope so!

So, there are laws to your relationship with money and laws to your relationship with love. One of the things I firmly believe is that the "honeymoon" never has to end. I believe in every cell of my body that the honeymoon never has to end, and it does end because we poison it with violence, aggression and everything else that we do in relationship to one another. There are ways to work with everyone's character, but you have to be willing to really work at it.

Love and money—both of those things are really serious, and yet they are not serious at all. You need to be able to laugh at yourself, because we are tragic individuals. Really pay attention to yourself for one day—how can you take yourself seriously? If I watch myself for one day, I am going to notice that every time I walk by a mirror, or anything that reflects, I am going to notice myself and preen a little bit. We cannot take that seriously because it's meaningless.

Our unconscious relationship to money is what allows us to be successful, and that success doesn't have a figure attached to it. The success or lack of success is the ease with which we are able to maintain relationship with the material world. That relationship is completely locked into our unconscious "script." We might be successful relative to money because of our karma—maybe we even find ourselves very successful—but if that creates so much stress that we have ulcers or migraines, then it is not success. Success with money is having money in relationship to the natural context of the Universe and its bounty.

We want to stop thinking of money in terms of having or not having it, and we want to start thinking of money in terms of having it without stress or worry, so that our relationship with money is natural and unproblematical. Someone once said that it is better to have loved and lost than never to have loved at all; that's true because every time we love, it builds something in us that creates truth, reality and an abiding relationship to the Universe. If you have ever really loved, something has been built in you that cannot be taken away, even when the body dies. Every time you have a conscious experience of objective beauty, something in you grows and progresses. That's why one of the recommendations in raising children is to expose them to a variety of experiences, because it builds something real in them.

Our lack of naturalness and ease in relationship to anything—love or money or whatever it is—is the result of our psychological script. Any response we may have to life that is not natural, that is not full of gratitude and presence, is hooked into the ego script. The chances are we are not going to be natural, and the life script has to be changed at its root.

My view of changing your life script is always relative to Yogi Ramsuratkumar. He knew what He needed to know, and He told me what He needed to tell me. Beyond that, everything else was unnecessary data for me. T.M.I.—Too Much Information. I love that! I could write that on most of the letters I get from students and send them back, but, being insecure, I've only written that on the tops of two letters! Too much information is too much information, and my time is limited. I cannot spend my time deciphering a fifteen-page letter, and if it's a fifteen-page letter, it's Too Much Information.

In relation to my Master, Yogi Ramsuratkumar, I didn't let my mind interfere with my work with Him . . . Look, I've been so fucking brilliant today, I don't know if I can keep going. I'm sure I'm going to fuck it up. So, without your permission, I'm going to end now.

ॐ

Always Make a Profit

Just by virtue of the fact that we breathe, we naturally take in more than enough energy every day than we could ever use. The reason we often find ourselves without the energy we would like to have is not because we don't have the energy; it's because we have spent the energy in uncreative ways. There are two kinds of stress: negative stress and positive stress. Positive stress is profitable for the Work and negative stress is not. An example of positive stress is when you're working on a piece of art, and you are so inspired that there's nothing but you and the art. You can even go for days without eating or sleeping. So that's an example of positive stress.

Negative stress is worry, obsessing about something, expressing rage. In principle, the approach to everything is to see things in the context of accepting what is as it is, and through that seeing, you shift your relationship to whatever it is you're seeing. On a very basic common sense level, the way we start is with some general categorization in our lives: what is the positive stress that applies and what is negative stress? Some negative stress is more subtle than others.

For instance, suppose one of our parents is an alcoholic, a drug addict or a criminal. This knowledge is tremendously stressful because we love our parent and maybe we try and protect them. If your father is is always traveling from

Colombia to America, and every time he comes back from America he's got tons of cash money, you say, "Dad what do you do?" "Oh, I sell coffee," you're in conflict. You love them and even want to protect them, but part of you thinks maybe it isn't coffee he sells but something less legal. That's negative stress. Sometimes negative stress is very subtle because we repress it and put our minds on other things; we try not to deal with it directly because we just don't know what to do with it. At other times we're concerned; we don't know what to do about our concern, so it's subtle.

The first step is some recognition of the difference between negative stress and positive stress. Positive stress brings energy in, negative stress wastes it away. Once we're able to come up with a clear label, we can stop a lot of the negative stress. It's just so deep and habitual that we're going to have to use the heavy artillery, but some of it we can just stop very easily. That's where it begins. If we eliminate all of the leakages of energy through negative stress, we're not necessarily going to be flying around; we won't suddenly have so much energy that we can't sleep.

Energy is meant to be used creatively or productively, we could say. One of the things that go hand in hand with stopping the wastage through negative stress is learning how to use the energy that we suddenly have in a creative way. One of the principles of energy is you can't just keep saving it, because it starts blowing circuits in your nervous system. So, you need movement, movement, movement. If you're used to having low energy all your life, then you're afraid of using it. If suddenly you have more and more energy, you want to save it because you're used to having low energy, and you want to have a savings account. It doesn't work that way with energy. The savings account is not in the physical nervous system; it's in the Universe. It's like having a bank account in Switzerland, and you need the number to get in the bank account—it's literally the same thing. You have a bank account with the Universe that is full of gold, but you need the number to get in.

I make every decision based on whether there is profit or no profit, gross or subtle—or we could say "spiritually," which covers all domains. For instance, someone wanted to move to Australia recently. There were three primary considerations: one was the couple and their kids, or the immediate family; the second was the extended family, or parents, brothers, sisters, aunts, uncles; and the third was the situation in Australia. I ask those three questions to make such decisions for myself; when students ask me, I ask them those same questions.

Let's say you live in Mexico City and you have children. Do you plan to be rich or not? If you plan to be rich and you have children, then to some degree you're going to live in fear in Mexico City. That's on the unprofitable side of the journal. That's the way I would look at it, but I don't know if that's true or not for you. Then the second part of the formula is: what's the energetic relationship to the extended family, and how much is it going to cost if you move away? How big is the family? How close is the family? How much suffering is it going to cause your mother? That's a real question.

That is the order of the three primary considerations: the first order of importance is your kids; the second order of importance is your parents. Not the other way around. Your parents took care of you, they raised you, they kept you safe—or not, as the case may be. They did their job; now you're an adult, you're independent. It's the same if one of my students has one parent left who has Alzheimer's and needs full time care. If they ask me, "Should I go out and live with them and take care of them?" the first question is, are they willing to move to Arizona so you can take care of them where you live? The second question is, "Do you have any brothers or sisters?"

In my scenario the Work comes before blood family. I was in my late thirties when I moved from New Jersey to our ashram in Arizona. All of my family lived on the East Coast. I'm an only child, and my father was dead, but my mother lived in New York City. She had a brother and sister who lived there, and we were all very close, but at the same time my mother and my aunt and uncle weren't my children. My mother had a really hard time with my decision. "What are you moving to Arizona for? It's so far away. When am I going to see you?" It was the same thing with my aunt and uncle, her brother and sister. We were very close, but now they're all dead; I don't even remember who they were, because I want them to just go on to wherever they're going to go. I don't want to be sentimental and have them hanging around trying to satisfy my needs in some ghost body, when they should be off taking incarnation again!

So, my family was really upset when I moved to Arizona, but moving was the profitable thing to do. I said to all my family, "My home is open, visit any time you want, stay as long as you want." The price was that some feelings were hurt and my mother was worried. There was some tension, but my mother was incredibly forgiving, so it wasn't a big problem.

I'm very committed to people supporting their blood family, their parents, brothers and sisters, aunts and uncles. I've sent students away from their home in Arizona for anywhere from a couple of days to years to take care of aging parents, to really bring a responsible relationship to their family—and, by my criteria, the Work comes before blood family. If there has to be a choice, the Work comes first. Sorry! Usually it never comes to that choice; usually there's no conflict between being responsible to one's blood family and the Work. Usually. That's the second level of profitability or loss.

The third level of profit or loss is: Is there something there for you that's profitable? It may be a professional opportunity, the difference in culture, climate or whatever. In the right spots in Australia there is some clean air—a nice breeze off the ocean, no pollution. That's high on the level of profitability. When you have a major decision in front of you, weigh those three questions when you're saying to yourself, "Well, I don't know. Should I even consider this thing?"

You know, this is a wonderful place to be, but it's Mexico City. All of your kids are only going to get older. So what if you have a possibility of advancing in your job? You're still going to be in Mexico City, if you know what I mean. That might be a profitable thing to do, but on the other hand maybe not. It's not likely to get any better here. What's likely to happen is the world economy is going to crash, nature is going to go ballistic, crazy, every active volcano is going to be blasting whatever it can. There are going to be earthquakes, tidal waves, tornados, draughts, floods—maybe not in our lifetime, but maybe, because some of you are pretty young.

I see America getting a lot worse before it gets better, politically speaking. Things are not likely to get better: a new president, a different government. The forces that move our sociopolitical system worldwide are a lot bigger than any one government or politician or organization. When the whole crash has gone through its cycle, then there will be the possibility of radical change, socially and politically, across the face of the Earth. That's my bad news scenario. On the other hand, it almost might be good news, because I don't see radical political change coming in America the way things are now.

Ted Turner is a man who cares deeply about the Earth and health. He's got a lot of money and years ago, as a way to kick the wealthy people of America in the ass, he donated a billion dollars to charity. He was hoping he would spark a movement. You know what? Nobody followed him. There was no movement because people are scared. They don't want to give their money to good causes so they can take care of themselves, just in case things get bad. People are scared.

On the profit side of the ledger, these are the factors you weigh when you need to make a big decision. If staying somewhere like Mexico City is profitable, then you figure out how to work around the negatives and you stay. If moving becomes profitable, then you figure out how to make the transition as graceful as possible and you move. To me it's all profit. Where's the most profit?

I was going to Germany and teaching before I started going to France. I had a solid body of German students who loved to practice. These people are tough, hard workers. I had a really great sangha in Germany with solid households, then I went to France for only a few years and bought an ashram. I had no French students. People were saying, "Hey, how did this happen?" The reason was that according to all of the divinatory systems in the world, France is divined to be one of the safest physical locations on the face of the Earth in the coming centuries.

Yogi Ramsuratkumar led me to France. It's very clear. We're established in France. We're doing well—we're even friendly with some of the neighbors. So, as I tell all of my American students, if the shit hits the fan, I'm going to France! You're welcome to come, but I'm not committed to living in America the rest of my life. We're building a new ashram in Arizona; we have two hundred acres of land out in the desert, and I'm moving forward as if nothing is ever going to change. But if things change, I can move tomorrow if I have to. Like Arnaud said once about his attachment, or detachment, to Hauteville:

"I can move tomorrow if I have to." I can move tomorrow if I have to, and I will. And I'm not coming to Mexico City—I'm going to France!

Everything has a price. It's like with any big move, if you know how to survive, you know how to survive; if you don't, you don't. If you're creative and able to survive here, you will be creative and able to survive anywhere; if you're not creative and you don't know how to survive, then you'll have trouble wherever you go.

When we moved from the East Coast to the Arizona ashram, we had a guy with a master's degree in city planning digging ditches on the side of the highway, and we had a guy with a master's degree in education, who was a math teacher, working in a post office sorting mail. But we did fine. We were surviving. People were creative and we had food to eat that was not always what we wanted. There were years when we literally lived on cabbage and potatoes because it was the cheapest thing in the supermarket, but we survived fine. Everybody was creative.

So if you're creative, you'll be creative anywhere. If you can survive where you are, you can survive anywhere. Switching from one profession to another—why not? If you're creative in the profession you're in, you'll be creative in the new profession. If you're struggling where you are now because all the opportunities seem to be evading you, and you think that by switching professions you're going to change that mood, think again.

It's all profitability—not money but profit for the Work. Where can the Work best survive? I'm an advocate for cowardice. I'm an avowed coward. I'd always rather run than fight. When I was a little kid I got picked on relentlessly, but I never got beaten up because as soon as somebody would start picking on me, I'd start to cry. What a pain in the ass! That was no fun, so they always left me alone. I don't get fighting back. It's not part of my equation. I've got no pride to protect. I'd rather eat my pride and stay healthy.

Some spiritual systems put you in the middle of a storm where there's the most tension, the most demand, and that's where you work and learn to adjust. I say, "Great! Let them do it." One of my students is a doctor in France who works in the middle of the gypsy slum in his city. Nobody else wants to serve the gypsies, but he's a very dedicated man. He really loves to serve and heal people, and he's very devoted. Two people came in on the first day he moved into his office; while he was examining one of them, the other guy cleaned out all the furniture in the waiting room. He's had his life threatened more than once, but he's totally devoted to serving people.

I have students who have worked with the mentally handicapped, the aged and infirm, or who are nurses or doctors in various fields of healing. They are dedicated to serving others. When things get bad, the people who are really sincerely devoted to helping others are going to stay and help others. If people who aren't already devoted to that kind of service are thrown into such a circumstance, they will complicate their attempts to help with complaint and worry and everything else. It's not the way I work.

Gurdjieff left Russia during a civil war to protect the Work when he could have stayed in Russia. When you read the way Gurdjieff got out of Russia—for example, he had to have two different sets of passports—you realize that he had skills such that he could have survived anywhere. He left Russia to protect the Work, not to save his life. There are fabulous stories of how Gurdjieff survived in Paris during World War II. The Germans had invaded France, and it was very difficult to travel and get in and out of the country.

There was a British woman who hadn't seen Gurdjieff for many years. She was missing her teacher, and at a certain point there was an opportunity to travel to Paris to see him. She knew that Gurdjieff had a very rare, expensive favorite kind of alcohol, so she somehow found a bottle in London. It was a treasure, and she took it to France to visit her master. When she arrived, she offered the bottle to him. He looked at it with great appreciation and said, "Oh, my favorite! Come, come, dear." He took the bottle to the cupboard and opened the door—there was a whole cabinet full of this liquor, along with caviar, chocolate and all kinds of foods that were impossible to get in the middle of the war. He just put the bottle with the other ones.

Gurdjieff could have gotten out of France during the war, but he didn't want to. Picasso could have gotten out of France too, but he didn't want to, for a very different reason than Gurdjieff. According to the biographies, nobody fucked with Gurdjieff or Picasso. The German officers used to go to the art galleries around Paris and just take whatever they liked. Nobody fucked with Picasso or Gurdjieff, because they had force, although for different reasons. Same force, different context.

I think Gurdjieff stayed in France because that's where the Work would be most protected—not for fifty years, but for hundreds of years. The way I view things is that we go in the direction of whatever is most profitable, and we don't always see the profit in our lifetimes. Sometimes something that is most profitable is going to profit our children, not us necessarily. That's the way I make decisions: what is most profitable.

ॐ

Obedience

What is obedience? It seems pretty straightforward to me. There are three levels of obedience. The overt level is when someone says, "I need this," and you go and get it. Then there's the subjective overlay that we place even on the most direct practice of obedience. For example, someone says, "I'd like a cup of coffee." We ask, "How would you like it?" They say, "Black with sugar." So we make the coffee and think to ourselves, "Black coffee with sugar is really good with some extra spice, so I'm just going to add a little cinnamon." That is not obedience. Obedience is in the exact, literal attention to details.

The second level of obedience is to understand, by having observed experientially, what serves the circumstance and be able to provide that. For instance, my entire willingness to teach revolves around the Sacred Bazaar now. If I'm hosted in Europe, I don't care where I sleep as long as I have the right circumstance for the Sacred Bazaar. If I sleep in an uncomfortable room, I can put up with it as long as there's room for the Sacred Bazaar; if I have a fabulous suite with a private bath and everything else but no room for the Sacred Bazaar, it doesn't work. I wouldn't reject personal comfort, but that is not the most important thing.

People are pretty simple. They aren't all that complicated. We can figure out what people want after a day or two of being in their company, whoever it is—a teacher, a partner, a child, a parent. It's pretty obvious what people like and appreciate. My mother, for instance, really loved to complain, and she never went to any restaurant more than once when she didn't complain about it. The first time the restaurant was good, and the second time she would complain about it. So when I took my mother out, I didn't look for new restaurants she hadn't eaten in; I looked for restaurants she'd been to before so she could complain. It made her very happy! All of those kinds of things are obvious. If we give someone red roses and they say, "Oh I love red roses! How did you know?" why would we give them yellow roses the next time? But we do, over and over and over again: "Oh let's try yellow, let's try pink, because *I* like variety!"

People mean well—there's no question about it. At the same time, if obedience is what is appropriate, then instead of trying to find something that will especially please, we should just be obedient. So the second level of obedience is that we observe the circumstance and, based on our experience, we have a sense of what is wanted and needed, and that's what we provide. Once we have an ability to accurately sense what is needed without being asked or told, and without definitions needing to be made, the third level of obedience is that we are able to provide what's wanted and needed.

One of the catch phrases of my work is, "Obedience to the Will of God." God doesn't usually speak to us, but there are laws of nature, laws of the Work, and laws of relationship; part of serving the Will of God is to learn those laws and obey them. One of the laws of the Work is the conservation of energy. There are two ways to conserve energy. One way is to not waste the energy we have, which we do through over-emotionality, negative tension and compulsive behavior.

Every year or two there's another popular diagnosis in psychotherapy—a few years ago it was ADD: attention deficit disorder. That's still popular, but one of the latest things is OCD: obsessive compulsive disorder. We like letters in America! We say, "Oh, you have OCD!" It doesn't sound as bad as "obsessive compulsive disorder." It's almost "cool"—in fact, it's very avant garde to have whatever is the latest rage.

I was watching a movie last year, and I saw this character demonstrating a certain behavior. Another character in the movie said, "You have OCD!" I thought, "Oh, I have that." I felt a little bad that I had never been in therapy for it! I've just ignored it and gone on about my life. Luckily none of the women I've been in relationship with knew what obsessive compulsive disorder was, so they left me alone! Otherwise, it would have been terrible. I would have heard, "You have OCD. You need help," over and over.

I've had ADD, OCD, I've been manic depressive and passive aggressive and a few other things. I just ignore it and go on about my life. That's the way I deal with things. I think most people could deal with their lives the same way I do. The best way of dealing with any of those neuroses is to just take your mind off it. In our school, if you're having a problem, we recommend that you sing show tunes. "To dream the impossible dream . . ." Almost nobody ever does it, because we love our problems. We don't want to just be distracted and go on about our lives. We want to *deal* with our problems. Not me! I want to pretend they're not there and go on about my life. If you pretend they're not there for sixty or seventy years, before you know it, they won't be there! You'll be dead and you won't have gone to any therapy—think of the time and money you will have saved!

So, obedience to God. What does that mean? It means understanding the laws of Creation and obeying those laws, like conservation of energy. One of the ways you can conserve energy is by not arguing when it won't accomplish anything to argue. Arguing eats up a tremendous amount of energy and rarely achieves the end result that you're looking for. So why argue, in whatever circumstances you are in?

There's a story about a thief in India who was stealing. At one point the police were after him, so he ran home and said to his wife, "You have to hide me because the police are after me." She said, "No, I won't hide you." He said, "Why not?" She said, "Because I never agreed for you to be a thief. I never supported you. If that's what you had to do, fine, but now you have to pay the consequences. I'm not going to take on your karma." Then the thief ran to his children and said, "You have to hide me because the police are after me." They said, "No!" He asked, "Why not?" When they gave him the same answer, he started to understand that his behavior actually affected a lot of people, not just him. As the story goes, he reformed and became a great saint. Those kinds of stories are wonderful, but they don't tell you that it took forty years!

Like in the Zen story of the monk who was in the monastery for twenty years. He was frustrated because nothing was happening, so he was leaving. He decided to leave the practice and go get a job. He was walking out of the zendo, and he kicked a stone because he was angry—twenty years of his life down the drain and nothing! The monk kicked the stone and it hit a big bamboo pole, which was hollow. The particular way the stone hit the bamboo made a certain sound—bup!—and he was enlightened. That's a great story, but they don't tell you that it took him forty years to actually understand and integrate what had happened in a way that made it useful. Everybody wants enlightenment, enlightenment, enlightenment, but what people don't understand is that enlightenment is absolutely meaningless without the context that allows that condition of consciousness to be useful in the human domain.

We don't all need to become philosophers, but there is something to studying and understanding how things work. In some forms of Christianity they say that charity begins at home. Obedience also begins at home, not necessarily meaning in the house but at the first level—at the gross level. Everybody wants to serve God, but they don't want to wash the dishes. We want to start working with the idea of obedience in the most immediate circumstance of our lives.

On the one hand I consider myself very fortunate, on the other hand not necessarily, because there are some things I don't know much about—for example, I never had a regular job. I always worked for myself, even from the very beginning. When people talk about their terrible boss, who is such a tyrant and they can't get along with him, I've never had that kind of experience. I never had a job that depended on my relationship with the boss. In the same way, I consider myself very fortunate that I was never in the armed services. When I was in high school, if someone was really a problem kid—a hood or a bully—the solution was always to send him to the Army. That'll fix him! And sometimes it did, because fifty years ago, if you went to the Army, you ate shit or you died.

In America, people get away with all kinds of things, because every major system in America caters to the lowest common denominator of consciousness. We have to have mirrors in the bathrooms in the Army so that women can put their lipstick on. Great, but when they had to change the laws so they could put makeup on, that's not so great, because in America now you can take an entire organization down because of one little anomaly. "Oh, the sergeant made me do extra pushups because he's homophobic and I'm gay and he doesn't like it." What's the problem? Do the extra pushups instead of whining, "I have been disrespected, and I need my honor to be reestablished by going to court and winning the case." What a bunch of stupid shit!

We went to see Camille Paglia when we were in California. Wow, what a dynamo! One of the social issues she writes about is date rape: young women go to college, join a sorority and go to parties where all they do is drink. Then she goes home drunk with some guy and he has sex with her. The next morning she wakes up and realizes, "Oh my God I've been violated! I need my honor redeemed." Hell, if a guy is low enough or stupid enough or desperate enough to have sex with a woman who's so drunk she's basically unconscious, that in itself is punishment enough!

Camille Paglia, a feminist who is pretty much hated by most feminists in America, says, "Look girls, if you're going to a party at a fraternity house half-dressed with no bra and your blouse up to here and the other half down to here, in pants that you had to be poured into when you woke up in the morning, what do you expect? Girls, helloooo!" You're dealing with a bunch of apes here, you know. The height of these guys' lives is Friday night when they take a pint of beer with a shot of whiskey in it, knock the thing back and go, "Ho, ho, ho!" These guys are studying law and medicine. Look out in a few years! You're going to go under the knife with these guys? They're going to be looking at your breasts while they're supposed to be taking your appendix out? You could be in trouble.

Part of obedience is bringing a minimal amount of common sense to your environment. Life is predictable. Instead of being naïve and assuming that life is going to be different for *you*, you need to have a sense of what's going on. People often say, "It's great to be a grandparent because you can do all the things you didn't do with your kids." Of course, they mean that in a positive way: you can spoil them and take them all the places you never took your kids because you didn't want to spoil them. There's a law of parenting, and there's a law of grandparenting. One of the laws of grandparenting is: you don't live with your grandchildren; your children live with your grandchildren. If you're with your grandchildren but you aren't in relative harmony with your children, the parents, then you're going to create more difficulties than benefits. So, conservation of energy! One of the main ways we conserve energy is not to waste it through stubbornness and anger and stress. The best way to not be stubborn and full of stress is to relax and obey the laws of the situation.

We have a community in which once a month we have what we call a "work weekend" on the ashram. People come and do whatever projects we have to do—painting the walls or weeding the garden or whatever it is. No one gets paid by the ashram for work they do; everything is basically on a volunteer basis. In the Gurdjieff system, circumstances are intentionally set up to create certain conditions. I don't work that way. I figure if my work has integrity, then there will always be more work than there are people to do it, and it will be the kind of work that allows people to get what they need to get, practice-wise. So, we don't have to worry about creating extra work, because there's enough work for twice the number of people we have to do it. When there's not a work weekend, people are encouraged to come to the ashram when they have a few free hours and just contribute, however they can.

In our community we recommend tithing, which is a contribution of ten percent of one's income to the ashram. About five percent of the actively committed students in the community tithe. It's a funny thing: the people with the most money are the people who tithe, not because the people with the least money can't—they can. Their relationship to money is one of the reasons they have so little money; they're in survival, they're scared.

It is common human nature that when people *don't* have to do something, they tend not to do it with the same level of responsibility. If somebody is going to lose their job because they're late a certain number of times, then they aren't late. They get to work on time. Nobody's going to lose their job at the ashram, because it's all volunteer, and we're happy to have them. But people show up late with no sense of responsibility, and there are no consequences. That's not everybody—some people are very responsible—but many do not pay attention in this way. I'm not going to kick them out of the school; I'm not going to punish them. There are no consequences—except subtle, energetic, karmic consequences. That's one way in which people are not obeying the laws of nature: they are compromising the laws of nature by saying, "Well, there's no consequences to being late, so why don't I just sleep a little later?"

Women always have things to do. We have a dinner date, we're sitting at the restaurant waiting, and the woman shows up a little later than we expected. "Where were you?" "Oh, I had things to do." "What things?" "Oh, just things . . . " You can never pin them down. "What exactly did you have to do?" Then they get very defensive. "I have my things to do." You know, I look in the mirror every time I pass the mirror and fuss with my hair. God knows why, from the looks of it, but I do anyway. I'll tuck it in on the side, it lasts about three seconds and then, poof! I do it anyway, every time I pass the mirror, but it doesn't take any *time*. What kinds of things take *time*? I don't understand it.

Because there are no immediate, obvious consequences, we think there are no consequences to certain actions. When we think there are no consequences, we aren't as responsible as we are when we're *forced* to be responsible because we'd lose our job or because there are severe consequences, whatever they might be. Let's use charity as an example: you don't give money to charity to stay out of hell, you give money to charity just because it's the right thing to do. You don't give money to a charity because you'll go to heaven if you do it, or you'll avoid hell if you do it; you give it just because it's the right thing to do. In the same way, you bring responsibility to your circumstance just because it's the right thing to do, not because you'll suffer consequences if you don't, or because the guru is standing over you with a big stick. You do it just because it's the right thing to do. It's lawful to be responsible for the things that are your responsibilities—that's all.

It's really a function of irresponsibility not to pay attention to those kinds of details. You may say, "Oh well, we're neurotic, we don't know ourselves, and we can't see ourselves." That's a weak excuse. It's true, but it's also a weak excuse. If you want to know who you are, get out a piece of paper, take an hour, write a few things down, and then you won't be able to use that excuse again. Who are you? Somebody who is always late. Oh gosh, how easy is that to remedy? Maybe it's not easy, because you have to *want* to remedy it. We had a woman living on the ashram who was *always* two or three minutes late to meditation, so we said to her, "Just set your alarm clock five minutes earlier." She did, and she was still always late. So you might say to yourself, it's not that easy to change a habit. It is that easy—it *is* that easy—but you have to really have your attention on it, that's all.

You have to follow the laws of nature. The first time we went to Germany, we went into the Black Forest, and there was no garbage on the path. My German students, who were young at the time, were very proud of the fact that they take care of the environment in Germany. Twenty years later, in one generation, it's totally different. You walk through the forest in Germany and there's garbage all over the place:

cigarette butts, styrofoam, plastic cups and all kinds of junk. One of the laws of nature is that if you mistreat nature, nature will mistreat you.

In the Gurdjieff teachings and many other traditions, the Earth is considered to be a living being with its own nervous system and its own consciousness—though not in the way we understand consciousness as human beings. The tremendous upscale in natural disasters, like the flood in New Orleans and the earthquake in Gujarat and so on, is the result of the Earth rebalancing and reharmonizing itself, because we have toxified it. If you eat bad food, you get a stomach ache, you get a fever, you shake, you throw up. That's what the Earth is doing. There is only so much nuclear waste we can bury in the body of the Earth without having a *severe* reaction on the part of the Earth. It's a natural law.

Maybe most of us and our families aren't working in professions that are burying toxic waste and polluting the environment, but each of us needs to simply pay attention in the immediacy of our own lives to following the natural laws. We do some recycling on the ashram in Arizona. When we're at the movies and we have some bottle or can that is empty, the tendency is to want to throw it away instead of taking it home and putting it in the recycle bin, because it's just garbage to us. It really takes some attention and a bit of effort to take the thing back and put it in the recycle bin. We might never get direct feedback that a lifetime of that kind of attention to detail has made a difference in the world. It's not like God is going to come to us on our deathbeds and say, "You know, you've really paid attention to details, and I appreciate it, and I'm going to reward you for that." But we can know inside ourselves that we are resonant with the laws of nature and we are doing the right thing.

Just turn the lights out. It took me twenty years of marriage and constant reminders to turn the lights out before I turned the lights out. I didn't have to be reminded to put the toilet seat down, because one night when I was very young, I went into the bathroom in the middle of the night and there was no night-light in the bathroom. I sat down on the toilet, and somebody had left the seat up. I never left the seat up after that. "Oh, that's what they're talking about. I get it!" That was a shock! So, you know, turn the lights off—a simple little thing. Why? Because you can't afford the electric bill? No, because it's a principle of nature to conserve energy, that's all.

The point of the Sacred Bazaar is to bring whatever degree of harmony and balance we can bring, in one small way, to the overwhelming imbalance that is everywhere today. When I first started teaching I used to say, "There's no such thing as karma. It's a rip-off. I refuse to talk about it." For probably twenty years I never, never, never talked about karma—action and reaction, or every action has a consequence. I still have no sophistication in the laws of karma; I have a vague sense of the movement of it, but in terms of details, it heats my brain too much to even think about it. Since I have known Robert Svoboda, who is an expert in not only the philosophy of karma but the actual physical realities of karma, I've felt I can take a little bit of liberty and talk about karma once in a while.

Make a list of all the things that you are very grateful for in your life: physical attractiveness, physical health, material well being. Even if you're sick, poor and ugly, maybe you have fabulous children! Whatever you're grateful for in your life, you have now because of actions in previous lives. The consequences of your actions then are these things that you are grateful for now—your health, your looks, your material well-being, your fabulous children. It's completely impersonal!

How many of you remember past lives? I don't remember past lives, but I'm incredibly grateful for my health. I don't know what I did in past lives to be so healthy this lifetime. I want to generate consequences in future lives that are going to be beneficial, not stressful and grief-producing and horrible, because we all have some of that. You don't want to end up being a mother in Iraq whose husband happens to be a terrorist: the soldiers come in, blow up your house, kill your child and you don't know why that is happening to you. You're one hundred percent innocent in this lifetime, and this is just happening to you; but sometime or other, one hundred or one thousand years ago, something you did generated that consequence. It's not random.

In one form or another you have found the Path. You have the possibility to understand these laws and act according to that understanding, so that when you die—when all your memories die with you—the consequences of your actions are going to show up, somewhere and sometime, in a way that is full of health and attractiveness and material well-being and sanctuary. I showed up in this lifetime completely unconscious, just a guy, and I've had great health for sixty years. I think, "Wow, thank you God!" But really it's my activity that some time or other has generated that healthiness.

Every act of kindness and charity that we generate is going to generate consequences for us sometime. Okay, in this life, in this consciousness, maybe we're not going to see the consequences. So what? We're seeing plenty of it now from another time. Look at your fabulous kids. Great karma! They don't know what they did to show up as your child, in this circumstance, with intelligence and beauty. They're just innocent.

Understanding the laws of nature and obeying those laws doesn't mean you're going to save the world or create peace in your lifetime, however you personally in some way, shape or form are going to receive the consequences of that resonance. That's the point. Werner Erhard, who founded the

Forum seminar system, was talking about ego when he said, "I'm the biggest egotist in the room, because I live in a way that's going to benefit me." He said, "I give, I sacrifice, I serve, but who's going to get the primary benefit of that? Me."

Obviously there are times when we have to turn a situation that could generate negative consequences into a situation that generates positive consequences. No matter how deeply we understand the laws of consequence, our lives are not going to be free of grief. Every life has something that generates sorrow, grief, heartbreak. That's life. So we have to take the circumstance and say, "What can I learn from this?" That's how to generate positive consequences from the circumstance that can go either way. Often we don't do the things that generate negative consequences consciously; they're completely unintentional. We're just unconscious, that's all. I look back at some of the incredibly cruel things I said and did to girls I was dating when I was in university. Oh my God! At the time I was just a randy kid, thinking about nobody but myself.

One of Yogi Ramsuratkumar's very close students used to say that Yogi Ramsuratkumar would lose His temper and yell at someone. Then He would feel so bad about it that He would call them back and say, "Are you okay? This beggar is so sorry, he doesn't know what he's doing. Is everything okay?" Not a week goes by when I don't feel like that many times. "Oh, I shouldn't have said that!" Most of us are the unwitting recipients of things we weren't conscious about. Being here on the Path, now we have the opportunity to be a little more conscious, to bring creative intention to our lives, moment to moment. It's very difficult. One of the things that touches me is when I see people relating to those who work for them with kindness and generosity. You don't have to treat them like human beings, because they are going to kiss your ass anyway to keep their jobs.

We were eating in a fancy restaurant in France once. We're sort of peasants, you know—we're not spiritual peasants, but we were the only people in the restaurant who were actually looking at the waiters and talking to them like they were people. The two people at a table sitting next to us looked at their food and occasionally at one another but never once throughout the whole meal said a word to the waiter—except when they had to. The waiter would come over and talk, and they would keep their heads down and bark out the answer. In the simplest circumstances, it doesn't hurt to smile at somebody or look them in the eyes when you're talking to them, because you're going to get the consequences of a simple gesture.

There's a great story of Gurdjieff going into a restaurant one day with some of his students, and he said to the waiter, "Why don't you have a drink with us?" The waiter said, "Oh I can't. I'm working, and it's against the rules." Every time the waiter would come in, Gurdjieff—who they say was very persuasive—would say, "I'll talk to the boss if you want. Come on and just have one drink with us." Eventually the waiter sat down, started talking and just bared his heart. His whole story just poured out of him, and Gurdjieff listened. When the waiter was done, he said, "Oh, I don't know what came over me. I'm sorry." Gurdjieff said, "Oh no! No problem! Don't worry." The waiter left, and Gurdjieff never saw that man again, but we have no idea what incredible benefits that man may have gotten. Who knows? You take it on faith. When you generate an act of harmony and balance, for even one second, you don't need to see what it's creating, because you will receive the benefits of it, absolutely!

With the laws of money, they say that it takes money to make money. That's true as long as you're using money according to the laws of money. If you aren't, then you spend a lot of money and you lose it all. One of the laws of money is *don't* take things on faith—always find out what something is going to cost you, especially if you're dealing with friends. You know, maybe you're making jewelry and you want to order a certain element for your jewelry. You go to a friend who says, "Oh, I'll get it for you wholesale." That's great, but if you don't ask what the price will be, if the order shows up and it's three times as much as you thought it was going to be, even if that person is being honest and not cheating you, you're going to think they're cheating you. If you ask ahead of time and the price is three times what you expect, then you can find out why and adjust your whole vision of the thing.

To be obedient to the laws of money, you *do not* want to take things on faith; with the laws of karma, you *do* want to take things on faith. Where money is concerned, you want to remember to ask as many reasonable questions as you can think to ask, like, "Has this ruby been heat-treated?" Then if they're going to be honest, they may have to say yes. So much turquoise, red coral and amber is not real anymore. If you don't know to ask, then you buy something that is supposed to be turquoise or coral or amber, but it's not the real deal. In India, as in other countries, turquoise is considered a very sacred stone. Different stones have different influences. There's a whole science of gemology, and the beneficial influence of diamond and ruby and yellow or blue sapphire are all different.

If you want to benefit from these influences, then you have to obey the laws that govern them; an object like a stone has integrity within itself. If that integrity has been tampered with, it's not the same influence. Most of you probably know the research that has been done with sugar pills, placebos; the mind can change the physical body in just in a matter of minutes. The mind can do extraordinary things—but that does not change the fact that there are influences. For example, astrology is a science based on natural laws, not a form of superstition. The influences of the planets, the moon and the sun may seem subtle, but they are real. The same holds true of all things. There is a difference between a genuine El Greco or a genuine Diego Riviera and a copy. Even if the copy looks exactly like the original, there's a different influence that the original carries.

So, when you want to be influenced by things in your life—by a certain stone that you wear in your jewelry, or by a work of art, or an antique or even a symbol—you want it to be real. In Katmandu there may be twenty thousand thangka painters and maybe ten good ones who know the true symbols. Outside of skill and art, one of the things that defines a good thangka painter from a bad one is the bad ones don't care if the symbols are wrong. Maybe the goddess is supposed to have a sword in her hand, but they forget and put an axe in her hand—that creates a *very different* influence. It's important that the details be accurate, because if the details are not accurate, then the influence that you're getting is not the influence that you want to get from Tara or Avalokitesvara or Vajrayogini or Varaha or Vajrakilaya or Padmasambhava or Maitreya or Kubera or whoever it is that the image portrays. So, you want to be obedient to the natural laws. With the laws of money, ask questions and don't be stupid. With the laws of karma, you want to take things on faith. That's part of being obedient.

ॐ

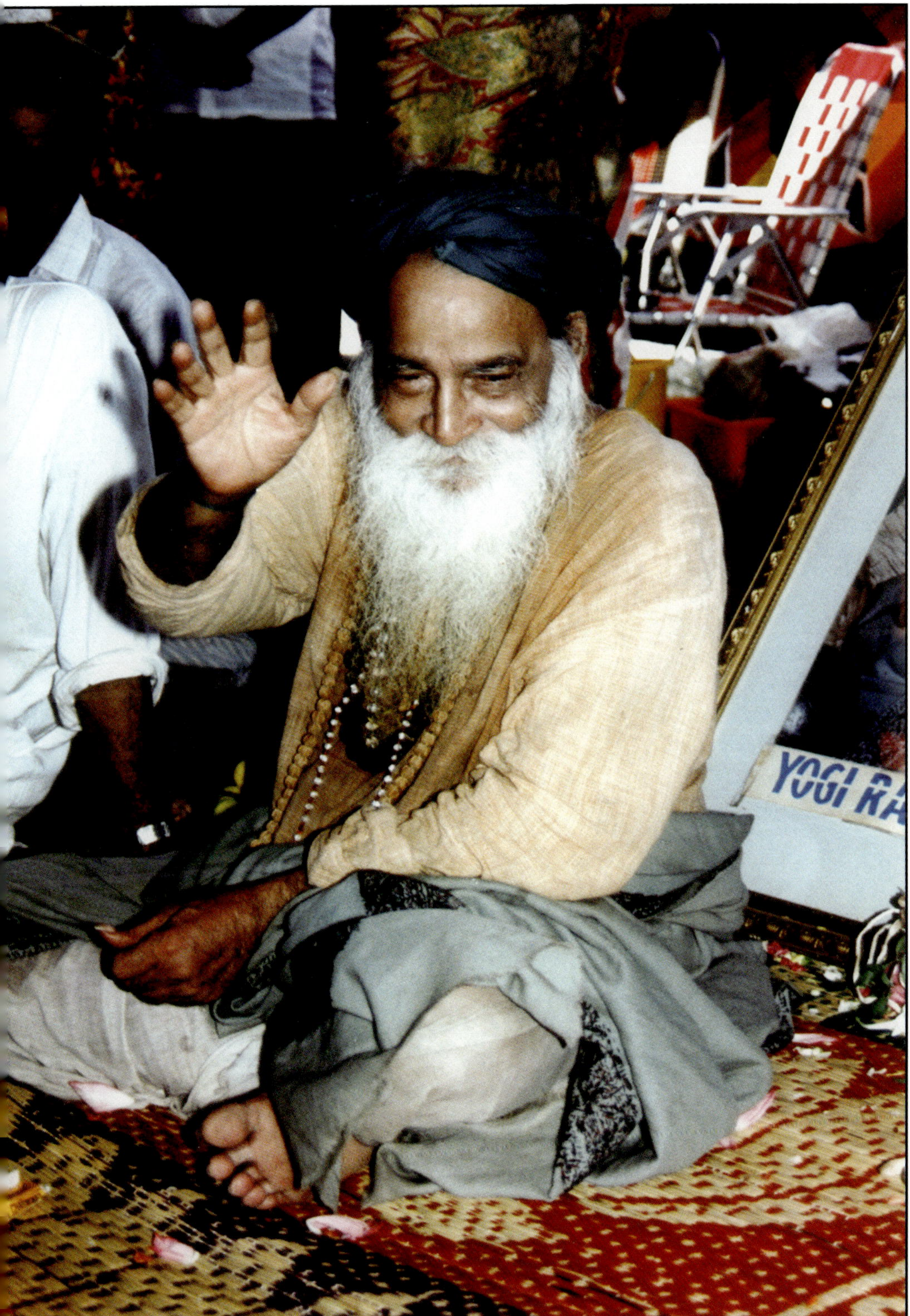

gi Ramsuratkumar.

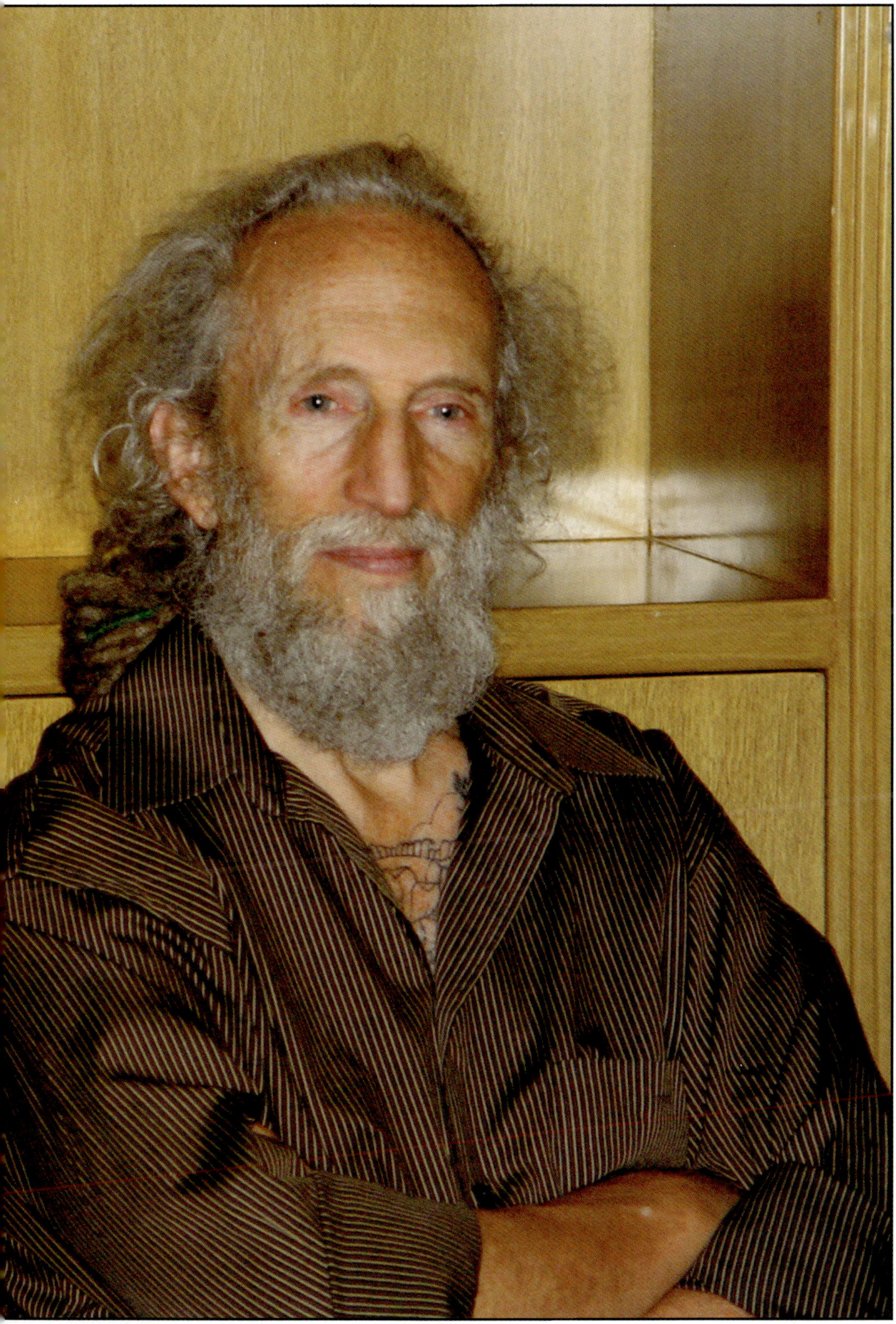

atural Arrogance.

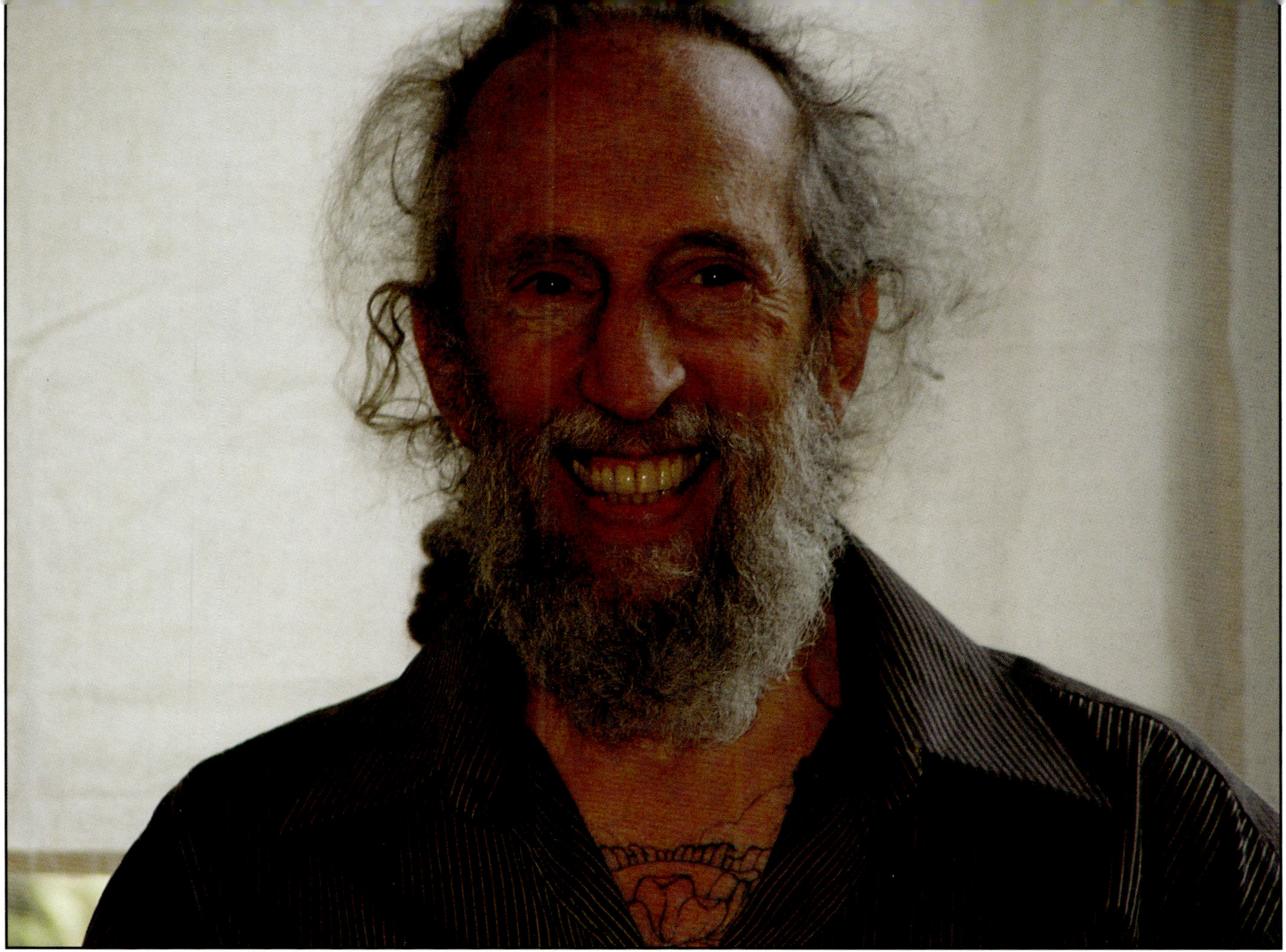

Nice Boobs.

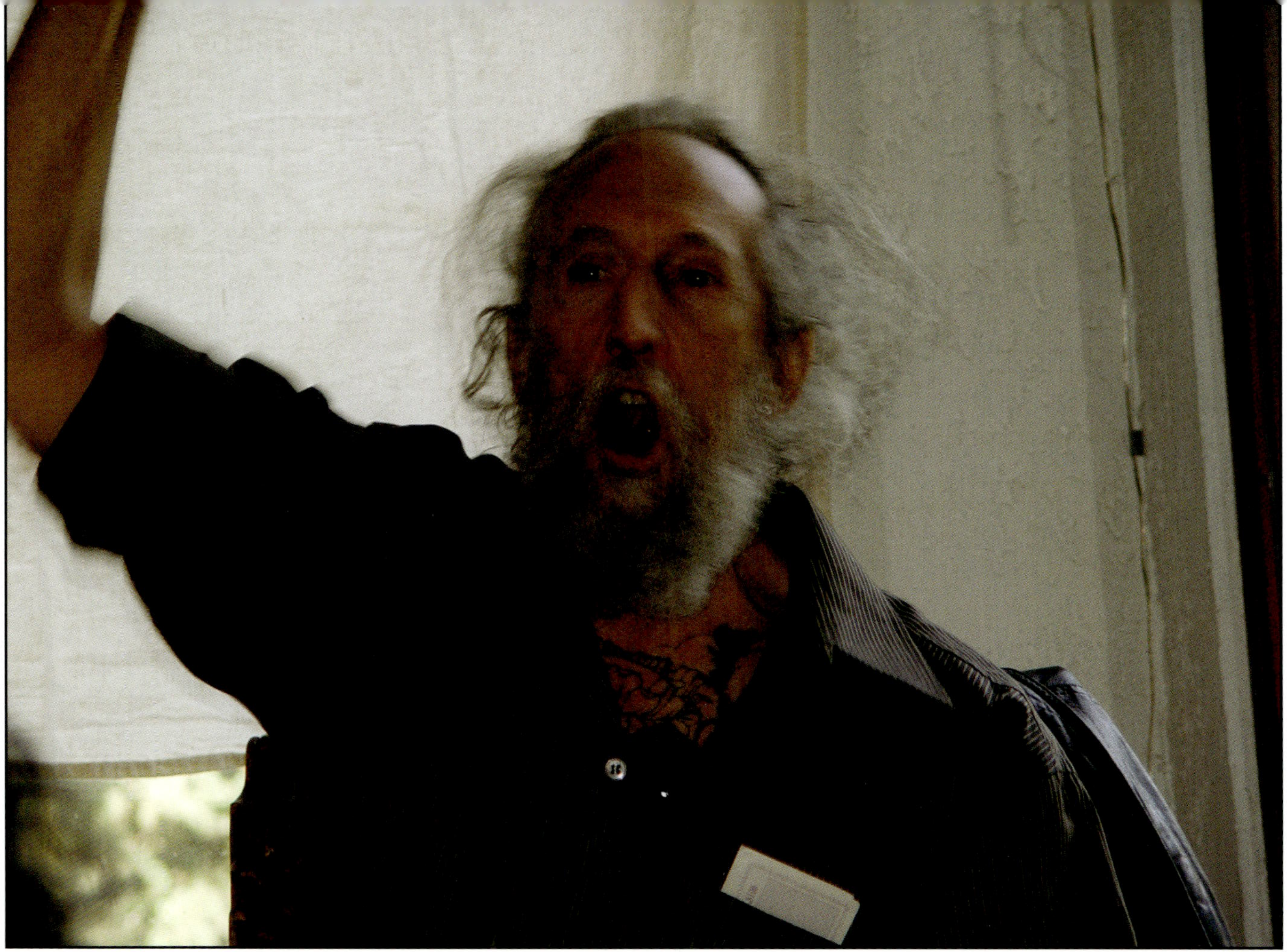

The Preacher.

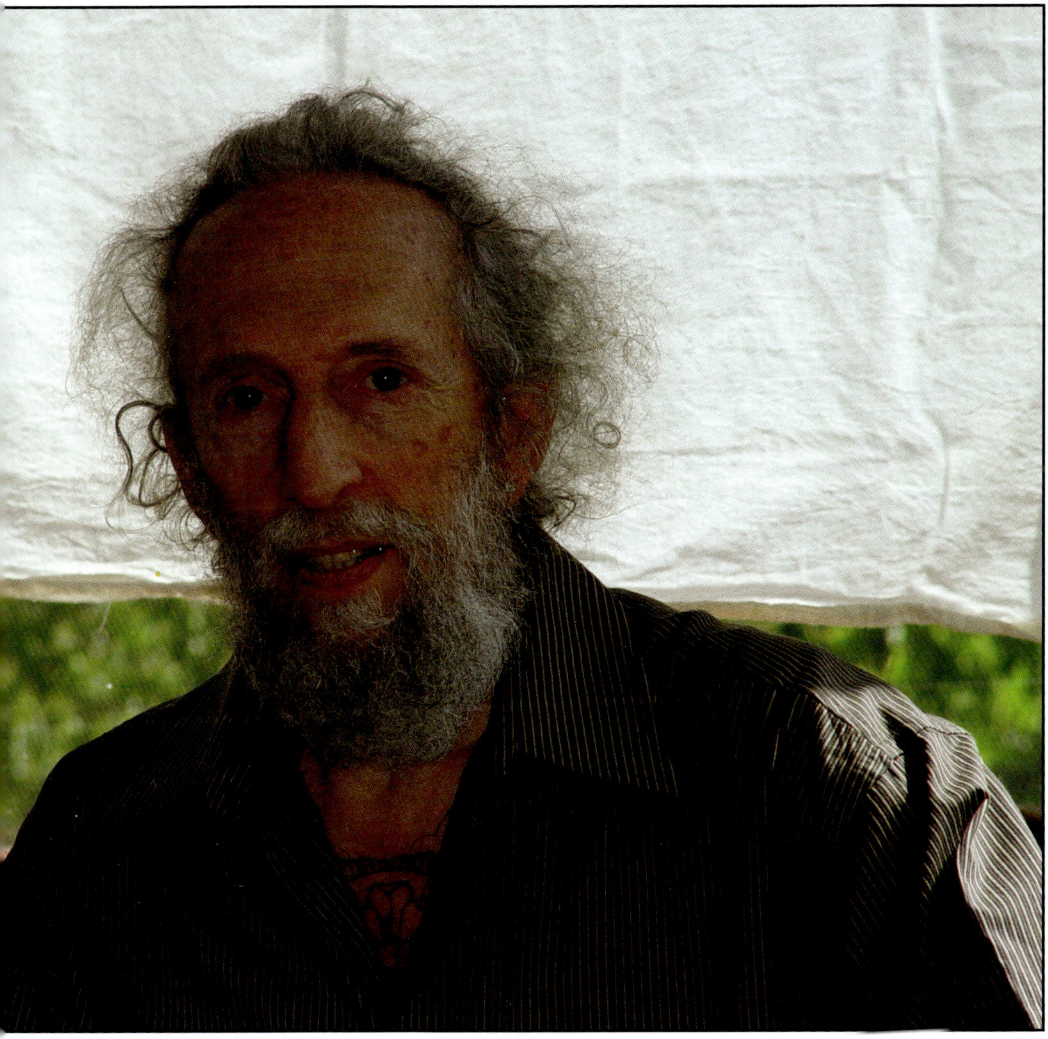

n the Verge.

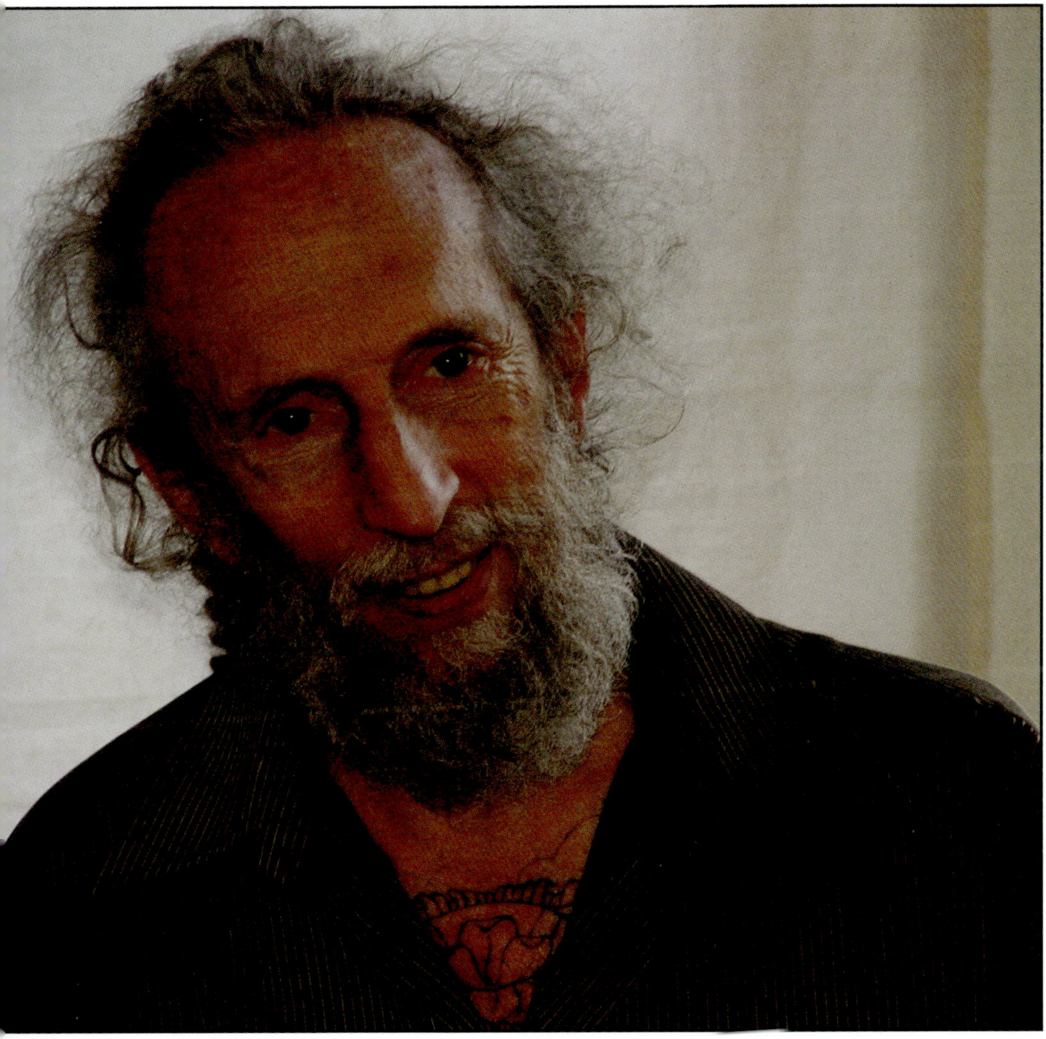

…st This.

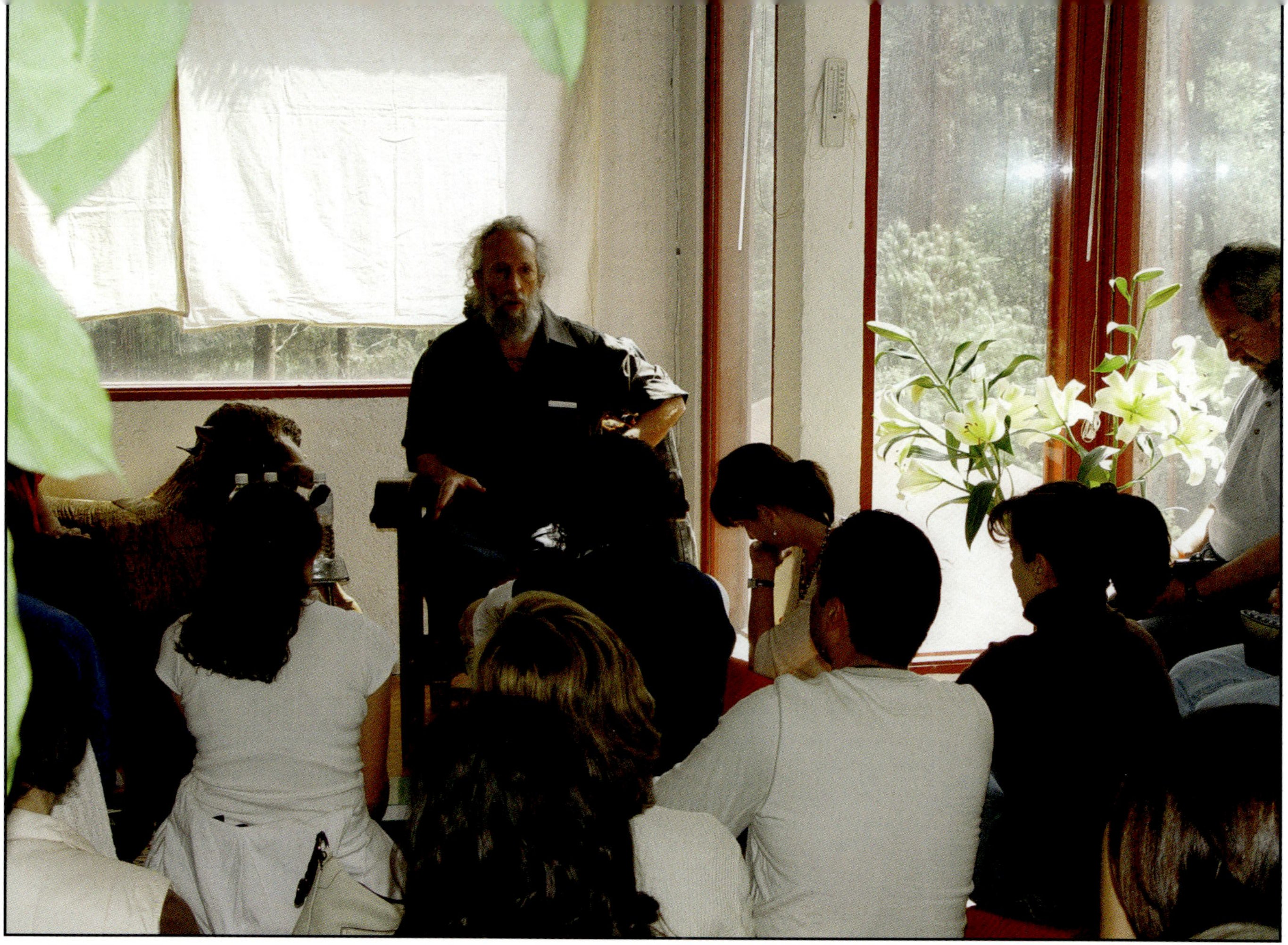

Group Shot.

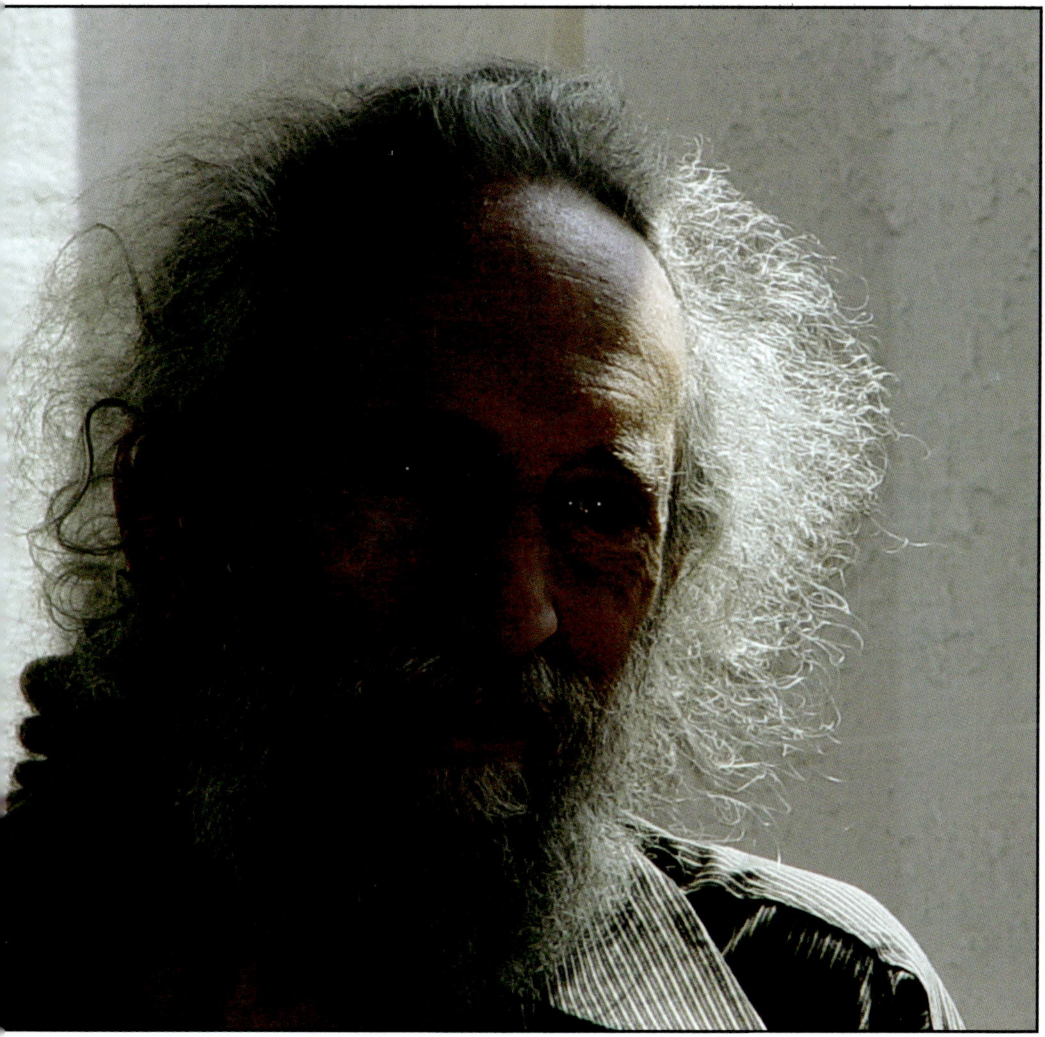

Job Well Done.

Hope and Hopelessness

There is a metaphysical principle which is: anything that we assume will happen before it is guaranteed to happen will probably not happen. For example, how many of you are artists? Someone looks at a piece of your work and says, "I want that," but they don't put money down or sign a contract. They say that they want it, and in your mind the piece is sold. How often does the person actually show up to buy it? Not very often, even if you're Picasso. When we assume something, we've already defined the energy, then we forget about it in a certain part of ourselves. If the possibility of it happening is not already concrete, most of the time it won't happen once we've assumed that it will.

Fears that we have—unreasonably ridiculous fears that something is going to happen—operate on a different principle. Fear is different than assumption, but hope isn't. Hope is not the opposite of fear; it's completely different. When we are hoping for something, we're actually assuming that that thing is going to happen, and that assumption is a very effective obstacle to the thing actually happening. We're all human; we all have desires, wishes, hopes, dreams—even just for basic health and security. So it's a very delicate issue to hold the possibility of something without actually crossing the line of assuming that that possibility is already concretized.

When we find ourselves hoping for something, there's nothing to do but just see that we're hoping for something and reestablish our intention to be in the present and hold possibility without weighing it down with our emotional desire. That's just a matter of attention and practice and remembering this principle: when we have assumed something before that thing is concretized, that assumption usually dispels or minimizes the possibility of it happening.

Yogi Ramsuratkumar used to say that when you invoke His Name for something, do it just once with faith and confidence. If you keep invoking His Name over and over, it means that you're not sure it's going to work. You're insecure, so you feel you have to reinforce it and that insecurity usually dissipates the energy, because there is a very real sense in which all of Creation is connected in an energetic network. Our prayer, our hope, our wish is not separate from the thing that we're hoping, praying and wishing relative to. Every subtle alteration in our own consciousness actually affects that thing. It's not like we're here and it is over there, in some distant place.

We all have our various fears. We have fear about our children being safe, car accidents, meteors falling on the house, our plane blowing up, or who knows what. I have a fear of fleas! When I was a kid I had outdoor cats that all had fleas, and they would come into the house. Sometimes I'd go to school and feel something on my forehead, and I'd have fleas jumping down on my face. I *really* have a fear of ticks—unlike dicks—that burrow into your skin. In France where we have our ashram there are lots of ticks. Lots of grass, very nice, it's green, it's very beautiful—lots of ticks! I never go outside and lie in the grass because everybody who goes outside and lies in the grass gets some kind of bite. Everybody says, "Do you want to go outside?" I go, "Ummm . . . I'm happy here."

When we are afraid that something is going to happen, that fear comes from a different place in our consciousness than our wishes for good things to happen. Actually, the more primal the fear, the more likely it is that it will not happen. If the fear is more of an adult fear, then it's more likely that something will happen, but most of our fears are irrational: fear of water, fear of heights. I remember the first time I was a young boy in Paris, and we went to the top of the Arc de Triomphe. My mother was saying, "Come on, look at that." I was saying, "No, I'm not getting near that edge." Even when I do get near the edge of something, I really hold on. It's completely irrational, because really, the probability of falling is insignificant. Although, somebody was photographing a boyfriend or girlfriend at the rim of the Grand Canyon in Arizona a few years ago, and they kept telling them to back up, until they backed up too far and fell off! That will sure ruin a honeymoon. Ordinarily, with those kinds of irrational fears, you're not calling the actual event into manifestation or avoiding it.

Back to hope. Hope is natural. It's like this: when you define any characteristic or quality, you automatically imply its opposite. You can't just hope. You can't under any circumstances have only one side of the equation. Things don't work that way. When there is hope, the implication is that hopelessness is there. You may not be feeling it or recognizing it, but it's there, and sooner or later you're going to hit hopelessness. Hope is natural to the human mind. To deal with hope *as it is* is to accept the reality of hope and the reality of hopelessness. It doesn't mean that hopelessness is necessarily going to manifest or overtake you, but it's there. The possibility of hope is the possibility of hopelessness.

For most of us, when we're committed to one side of the equation, we're resisting the other side of the equation. If someone is sick and you're praying for them to get well, it means you're resisting them not getting well, or getting worse. When you accept the reality that there is hope and hopelessness in the dualistic world, it completely harmonizes the energy that you've constellated around either of those two positions. When the energy is harmonized, it takes away the implications, the consequences. It simply leaves it as it is. Then there is hope, there is hopelessness, and what arises, arises.

If you have a ninety-year-old parent who gets sick, and you love them and want them to live, you need to realistically consider that they could die. They're ninety years old; their body is not as strong as a thirty-year-old. Whatever illness they have is much more strenuous on the body than if they were thirty, forty or fifty. So you wish for them to recover and live, but you also want to seriously consider the possibility that they might not. In our system, which is theistic, we would say that to harmonize in that way, to accept the whole thing as it is here and now—not just a little bit of it—is to turn it over to God instead of taking it into your own hands. Then, what actually comes to manifestation in the physical world is divinely ordained instead of mentally created by the force of our efforts.

For instance, if you work in the field of psychosomatic medicine, it's very clear that the mind can actually mold the physical world according to its own image. There's a system of Buddhism that involves repeating a chant for anything you want: money, a new house, love, whatever. You just repeat this chant and it happens. That doesn't mean that the manifestation you are chanting for is resonant to the Divine Will. It means you've just used your mind to mold Reality, like a sculptor. If you have a strong enough mind and enough energy, you can spend your whole life avoiding Reality by molding it to suit your own vision of things, your own purposes. If you're doing that in a positive way, that's not so bad—it's not Reality, but it's not so bad. But you also can do it in a negative way.

I was very devoted to the Silva Method when I was in it. People would say, "Are you going to do this all your life?" I'd say, "Why not? It's a good method, it works . . . Sure." It is a great method in its own domain, but its domain is very narrow and limited. One of the techniques is to close your eyes and repeat certain sayings over and over to program the mind, for example, "You can only use this technology for the good of mankind." That's a nice sentiment. Unfortunately it's not true.

A couple of things intercepted my teaching of the Silva Method that completely altered my view of it. In my own research I discovered how to use the technology destructively instead of creatively. I never did use it destructively, and I when I discovered that, I coincidentally decided that I needed to discover what was beyond a system in which you could use the energy creatively or destructively. That was one of the primary catalysts for my resigning as a responsible instructor in the system. Even when what we're creating with our minds is positive, it's still not the real thing. The real thing is what the Universe would produce under any given circumstance, not what our minds would produce under any given circumstance.

When you accept what is, as it is, across the spectrum, essentially you are turning life over to the Divine. You're essentially moving out of the realm of your past and the possibility of your future, in terms of how it affects your consciousness, according to the way you want it to fall out. You are basically saying to the Divine, "Okay, You move things. You create." Under that circumstance hope may still arise, but it is arising in a system in which whatever arises falls into the same category. It arises; you notice it; it subsides.

The way we usually are is that something arises, and if it's something that we want, we immediately grab hold of it. Then we are taking over the work of the Universe. When we accept what is, as it is, here and now, we have disengaged our spatial and temporal relationship to duality—which is always a function of the past or the future, of hope or fear—and we just surrender to the Universe. Many of us have that experience for a moment, and we know that we're completely free here and now. Then, all of a sudden, in the next moment, we realize that we're trapped again, and we say, "Oh, how did that happen?"

The Dalai Lama and other wise people say that you just keep practicing, and every time you have one of those experiences you are building momentum behind the experience. You just keep going. When you're accepting what is as it is here and now, qualities don't disappear. What disappears is your judgment of qualities—the ego's judgment of qualities. Hope will still arise.

It's natural to look at your children and spontaneously have a feeling that you want them to be happy and successful and healthy. When your kids start to bring home boyfriends and girlfriends, it's natural to look at their boyfriend or girlfriend and have some opinion. Some of our children are not so lucky. We have a long learning curve. Some of us need to have a lot of bad boyfriends and girlfriends before they figure out what a good one is like. And since most children have been abused by their parents in one way or another, most boyfriends and girlfriends are abusive. What else do they know? If you're a boy and your father drinks too much, and as a young child you observe your father fighting with your mother, you're going to have one of two responses: you're going to exactly duplicate that behavior with your girlfriends when you get to be a teenager and older, or you're going to be so turned off and shocked that you bury it. You may not treat your girlfriends that way, but you're always going to be relating to them through a veneer of fear, because you're going to be afraid that you're going to treat them that way. In either case you're not being genuine.

The ideal scenario is that we accept what is, as it is, here and now—to use the phrase from Swami Prajnanpad—and in that moment there is only the Divine. When we find ourselves back in the ordinary world of ordinary illusion and suffering, then we just keep practicing. We remember the moment of freedom and clarity, and we just keep practicing. There's no magic pill, unfortunately. No LSD or MDMA. If you take anything that looks like a magic pill too many times, you're left with very few functional brain cells.

Like Viagra. I think most people would be happy just to be over the whole sex thing. What do they want to extend it for? Now they have a pill for women that inflames their sexual desire. What for? The ideal situation is both the man and woman get tired of sex at the same time, and then they're a perfect couple for a change. Then they can just sort of settle into a relaxed life with one another, focus on good food and art.

We don't know the side effects of that kind of drug or the ones that relax everybody—like Prozac. Everybody's doing it. There's so much Prozac used in England that all of the water has Prozac in it, because the water is recycled, and there's no sun. It's a miracle if they have a sunny day in London every once in a while! People live all their life with no sun, mostly rain and gray clouds—it's very disturbing to the physical system. We're like plants; we may not be making chlorophyll, but we need the sun. The sun is a very important physical element in our lives. Every once in awhile somebody actually does make chlorophyll from the sun, and they turn green and then everybody else thinks they're from Mars!

I'm glad some of you are laughing because sometimes when I say something, I'm afraid everybody's going to take me seriously. That's actually why, when I talk in India, I almost never make jokes. When I first started teaching I had a great sense of irony and satire, so I wrote a satire piece about meditation. I think it was called "Meditation Techniques for Instant Enlightenment," or something like that. It was so obvious to me that it was a satire that I didn't think I had to say it was a satire, so we published it in a little booklet and started to distribute them. I was sitting in a meeting one day, and somebody asked me a serious question about the technique. I said, "Oh my God. This person doesn't know it's a satire." So I recalled all the booklets we had published and took them out of circulation. That was one of my first lessons as a teacher in the naiveté of many people.

So, we want to allow our lives to arise as they arise naturally in perfect resonance with the Will of God, or with the arising of the Universe as it is. If I can be so pretentious as to speak about the teaching of Swami Prajnanpad and Arnaud Desjardins, one of the classic errors that people make when they discover the practice, "accept what is, as it is, here and now," is that they turn it into a practice of separation. They unconsciously think that to accept what is, as it is, here and now, applies only to them as a separate being disconnected from all of Reality. In the beginning, of course, that's how you relate to it because you're dealing with you as you are, not what is, as it is. You're dealing with your habits and neuroses, not just your "yes" to life, but your "no." As Daniel Morin said a few years ago, you have to say "yes" to your "no" before you can deal with the "no."

The technique is "accept what is, as it is, here and now." It's not, "I have to accept myself the way I am here and now." It is "accept what is, as it is, here and now." To accept what is, as it is, is ultimately to accept the fact that there is no separation. What arises individuated as you is not separate from what is arising as the Universe in its ongoing process of creation, sustenance and disintegration—which is the same as the Father, the Son and the Holy Ghost, or Shiva, Brahma and Vishnu. There is also a creator, a sustainer and a disintegrator in Qabala, on the Tree of Life. If we have an aim, ultimately it is to simply allow what arises to be completely natural and undivided from what is as it is universally.

ॐ

Transformation

How do we change the roots of intelligence? We do a number of things. We pray a lot, and sometimes we get lucky, but part of the foundation of any spiritual path is an accurate self-knowledge. Essentially, in order to allow the full extent of Divine Influence in our lives, we have to open the doors of ego. Divine Influence is always active, moving, present and blessing us. Even if we can't open the doors of ego, just the fact of being in the field of blessing is already going to bring plenty of benefit. Just as in ordinary life, without the Path or any understanding whatsoever, when you live a number of years and have more life experience, you grow wiser. So too on the Path, even if you do nothing but simply stay in the presence of the Influence of the guru, you will have some benefit and progress.

E.J. Gold says that ninety percent of the Path is staying in place—just hanging in there. Metaphorically speaking, the way we process input, impressions or feedback that we get is to chew, swallow and digest that input. Obviously you can't eat all day long; you eat when the body is ready to eat again. It's the same with the Work. The amount of time—which could be lifetimes—between great feasts varies between individuals, depending upon our strength of digestion, our facility and so on. Weeks, months, years—it depends on the person. So when we are bored and feeling itchy for something new and exciting, it's good to know that ninety percent of the Path is just staying in place: standing in the Presence of the photographs, the murtis of the lineage, the artifacts, the books we read. Staying in the Presence.

One of the things that helps us get back to the roots of things is to have clarity about our motives, our actions, our process. For example, if we feel that we are not getting the love we think we deserve from our parents or our family, it's very common to displace that love onto something else like food, toys, pets, money or sports. As we get older we forget that we've made that displacement, then as adults we have this tremendous compulsion to accomplish something that we think is for the sake of art or for the sake of justice or to take care of our family. Really our drive to accomplish is for none of those things; it's to get love. Obviously people who are bulimic or anorexic are trying to use food to accomplish something. Of course, food can't accomplish what it is they are trying to accomplish, so it is a constant cycle of frustration and suffering. We are often full of these tensions that we attribute to certain causes, but the causes we attribute our tensions to are almost never accurate. So, the more clearly we can understand our own process the more likely it is we are going to be able to get back to the roots of our own intelligence.

G.I. Gurdjieff talked a lot about what he called "self-observation." He said that one of the keys that open the lock of denial and self-ignorance—of unconsciousness of self—is the body. In contemporary Gurdjieff work, they always start with the body first when working with self-observation of all the little habits we have. For example, every time we sit down at the table and use silverware, we always move the knife and the fork just exactly so. Every time we get in the car we move a certain way to get comfortable; we do exactly the same thing all the time.

We start noticing those things, and we don't make any judgment about them. "Oh wow, I'm really a creature of habit. I have no control over this!" We just notice them. Over time, self-observation starts to give us the idea that we are not as independent as we think we are. We discover that we are not just creatures of habit; we are actually puppets. That's a little shocking for most people, which is a good thing. In the Gurdjieff work they say that there is shock that is useful and shock that is harmful, or that there's stress that is actually useful and there's stress that just breaks things down and creates illness in the body.

Once we start to really get this idea that we are not as independent and in control as we thought we were, that automatically creates a deeper self-reflection. We start looking at the kinds of things that we completely take for granted. Most of us think that we get up in the morning, go to the closet and randomly pick out some clothes to wear, but actually it's not random at all. Different colors have different influences, and often we'll pick a color we are going to wear because we have some unconscious process going on.

Then we start looking at our thought process. A lot of decisions we make are made without ever thinking about what's stimulating that decision. For instance, sometimes you meet someone and have an instant rapport, and at other times you meet someone and have an instant negative reaction. I met someone the other day, and I was having a little negative reaction. When it was time to say goodbye, I didn't stand up. Everybody else was standing up to say goodbye, and I just stayed seated. A second later—literally a second after I didn't stand up—I realized it was because I was having this unconscious response. Because of my failure to resonate with this person, I wasn't going to honor him by standing up and saying goodbye. "I'm the boss and you're not, so kiss my ass," was what I was saying. The point is that my behavior was not spontaneous.

When we start to recognize that the little choices we make during the day are completely conditioned by something in our unconscious, it stimulates an even deeper investigation. One of the most useful pieces of information about transformation or self-knowledge is that, metaphorically speaking, there are a series of doors and rooms. You can't start in the last room; you have to start at the first room, then go into the second, the third and the fourth. Every door is locked. Every room is locked. The only key we have is the key to the first room, then the key to each consecutive room is in the previous room. So, we open the first room because we have the key, and the key to the second room is in the first room, and so on. If we are willing to look for the key in the room we're in, we'll find it. Sometimes it's obvious, and sometimes it's hidden away, but the key to the next room is always in the room that we're in. We don't need a whole program. All we need is the next step, and if we take that step, within the taking of that step is the key to the next step, and so on and so on.

The first thing you learn in martial arts are basic moves—basic blocks, strikes, rolls. In developing competence in those basic things you automatically are brought to the next level of physical achievement. So in aikido, which is a very fine form of martial arts, one of the things that you have to do to advance at the higher levels is to teach what you've already learned. It's not learning more throws or greater speed or more intuition; teaching what you already know is the key to the next level of advancement.

Sometimes the process is very linear and obvious and direct, and sometimes it's a very around-the-corner kind of thing. The way it usually works is the farther you advance—the more deeply you have insight into your own process—the more obscure the Path becomes and the more hidden the key to the next room is.

I have been teaching for thirty years. If we want to include the time I taught metaphysics in the Silva Method, we could say thirty-five years. Metaphysical laws are a very good foundation for the spiritual Path. In the beginning, when I first started teaching I was very naive, as we all are at the beginning of anything. I thought that the Path would be very easy, and that all my students would immediately understand what I had understood and that would be that—within a few months they would be finished and we'd all go on vacation! Thirty years later, that naiveté has been seriously frustrated!

There are several different ways to approach transformation in the spiritual traditions. One way is through heroic practice: You go out in the mountains, sit and meditate for twelve hours a day. You don't sleep, and if it's freezing or burning hot, you don't wear clothes. Who cares? Meditate! That's one way: heroic practice. Another way is through what we could call purification: You have a very clean diet, you only wear clothes made of natural fibers in light colors, you don't go to movies that are going to excite your desires. Everything is very calm, very gentle, very soft. That's another way, which is not particularly the way I would recommend, because you have to give up coffee and chocolate and all that! And you have to give up Bruce Willis movies . . . Forget it!

The other way of transformation is called guru yoga. In guru yoga you give everything—all of your attention—to the guru. You completely surrender everything internal and external—all choice, all decision, all independence—to the guru. Then the guru takes care of everything. Now that's a very tricky path, because if you pick the wrong guru, you're fucked. So you have to pick the right guru, and there are a lot of wrong gurus out there, as evidenced by all the scandals these days.

I met my guru, Yogi Ramsuratkumar, in His physical form about a year and a half after I started teaching; I met Him subtly before that, but I didn't know it consciously. It took me about four years to figure out that He was my guru. I was, and still am, very arrogant. I felt superior to everybody and everything, and I was very independent, so it took me a while to figure out that I wasn't the master—I had a master.

In the beginning, my path was the path of heroic practice every day. I was a lot younger then, which helps. If you're going to meditate six hours a day, it helps to be in your thirties! Plus I did a lot of other stuff—it wasn't just meditation but also breathing, concentration, yoga. My personal tendency was to practice hard, and when I started teaching I expected my love of practice to inspire my students to practice with equal heroism. Boy, was I wrong! Not that I don't have some students who practice with tremendous discipline and integrity—I do—but heroic practice is not a hallmark of my student body.

There is a story about three great Sufi teachers who were taking incarnation to teach. They were in heaven with Allah, and Allah said, "There are three of you, so we're going to divide humanity into thirds. The first shaykh is the most advanced, so he gets the first choice of disciples." So the shaykh surveys humanity and takes the best third to be his disciples. Then the second shaykh looks over humanity and he takes the second-best third. The third shaykh looks at what's left, and he faints!

When he wakes up Allah says, "Well, we'd better send you for some more training." So Allah sends him back up to heaven for six thousand more years of training. After six thousand years, the shaykh comes back to earth; he looks at the third of humanity who have no path yet and whose teacher has not incarnated, and he faints again. So Allah sends him back for another six thousand years of training. Finally the shaykh comes back again, and by this time he's ready to make the sacrifice and take on the responsibility.

Llewellyn Vaughan-Lee told me this story; he's in the lineage of Bhai Sahib and the Naqsbandi Sufis. He said that the third shaykh in the story was their grand shaykh, who started the Naqsbandi Sufi path. He said, "And so we say in the Naqsbandi path that we have the worst disciples but the best methods, because our shaykh had twelve thousand more years training!" I think he told me that because we feel the same way: the worst disciples but the best Yogi.

So, in guru yoga the process is to completely trust the teacher, but to be successful in that Path you have to know who the teacher is. If you define the teacher by the human being who is representing that function, then you've completely missed the point, because the human being that represents the function is divinized in a certain way but also still has bad habits and neurosis. Sooner or later every one of us who has a teacher is going to come up against something in the teacher that we feel diminishes their integrity as a teacher.

In my school, I never asked for money from my students before the Sacred Bazaar—a little bit for books, you know, but nothing substantial. All of a sudden the Sacred Bazaar comes along and people are looking at some really expensive antiquities. I don't even bring the pieces that are the big bucks, but they're there. A number of my students were asking, "Oh my God, is Lee just a businessman?" Some people were really upset. They couldn't figure out how I had changed so dramatically after being so humble and so, "Oh, don't worry about the money—if you don't have it, don't pay." Suddenly it was, "This piece is two thousand dollars—pay me."

Some people had big problems with it. Some didn't. Some thought it was fabulous: "This is great!" All of my students who now have environments that are filled with incredible beauty that they never had before are very happy. I usually don't bring the big pieces to the Sacred Bazaar either. I have big stuff—stone pillars that are two and a half meters tall and weigh about seven hundred kilos. They are seven hundred years old and full of carvings of Vishnu and all of Vishnu's playmates. All of a sudden these kinds of things are showing up in people's apartments. Wow!

That's what created doubt about the teacher's integrity for some of my students. For other teachers it's other things. There was one teacher in America who was a celibate monk for twenty-five years. He went to Hawaii one day to teach and came back with a woman. He told the community, "Oh, I've seen the light. I was trying to teach alone, and now I realize that every king needs a queen, and this is your queen." Then the "queen" started acting like Eva Peron, and as you can well imagine, the community didn't take well to that. Three weeks after he got back to the community, he realized he'd made a big mistake. He got rid of the queen, but a lot of students left in the meantime. They felt that they could not continue to feel confidence in their teacher after that.

One of my students, Purna, is teaching, and I think it's working out very well. The first time I visited his ashram, in a moment of devotion and ecstasy, Purna said, "This is Lee's ashram, this is not our ashram. If Lee wanted this ashram I would give it to him right now, this minute." I am not the kind of person who would take him up on such an offer, even as a challenge, but some gurus would say, "Oh great, this is much nicer than my ashram, I'll take it." I think Purna meant it. I don't think he was saying that to be somehow spiritually correct, so that's very good—even if he was quaking after he said it.

Whenever I think of some of my students teaching it worries me, because in the Sufi tradition they say that if the teacher gives a teaching absolutely correctly, with total integrity, but the student misunderstands the teaching and acts on the basis of that misunderstanding, and that action creates some negative consequences, the student pays for the negative consequences once, but the teacher pays for the negative consequences twice. In turn, if the student passes on the misunderstanding to someone who acts in a way that creates negative consequences, that person gets one negative consequence, the student gets two negative consequences, and the teacher gets four negative consequences. So it always worries me when I think of any of my students teaching, but not so much that I can't sleep at night. Going unconscious is one of the greatest things in the world—I can always sleep! So, when Purna made that offer it was very gratifying to me because that speaks for his reliability as a good student—I can relax a little bit.

As my teaching work has gone on over the years, through the blessings of my master various technologies for transformation have been revealed to me. The thing I most want to do is pass those technologies on, but with the agreement or understanding that those technologies will not be misused. As the years have gone on, and I've seen how easy it is to misunderstand, and then based on that misunderstanding, misuse the technology, I have become more and more conservative relative to how much I give. Inside I am giving two hundred percent, but outside I am more conservative. I have started saying to my students, "Well, we're just not going to be a heroic practice school, so let's just say we're doing guru yoga." There is still plenty of space and opportunity for anyone who *wants* to practice heroically, and I have plenty of gifts I can give—plenty of technology and instruction.

My master, Yogi Ramsuratkumar, had a tremendous degree of trust in me, but it wasn't absolute in the beginning.

He would watch me—not just physically, because I was only with Him two weeks a year. He watched me over the twenty-six years of our physical relationship, and little by little He relaxed, because I proved my integrity and my capability to Him. Slowly, my relationship with Him moved from one of heroic practice to one of guru yoga. I am not a great student; I am a fair student. I am too uptight and defended to trust anyone, even my master, one hundred percent, but I'm a pretty good student. So consequently, His gifts to me were parallel with the degree to which He could trust me to understand correctly and to use what I understood correctly, so that I wouldn't drag Him back into incarnation to pay off negative karma for my mistakes when He was ready to go on and get the hell out of here.

One of my students who was living on our ashram left. He didn't leave the school, and he wasn't in any way challenging his devotion to me, but he did leave the ashram—and he was a really pivotal person on the ashram. Guess what the catalyst for his leaving was? A woman. I was visiting with Mr. E.J. Gold, and he said, "What's new?" Whenever there's a really incredible teaching opportunity E.J. always knows it, and he always knows the right question to ask to kind of bring it up. So he says, "What's new?"

I was thinking, "I don't know. Nothing's new. Everything's going along fine." I had to say something, so I said, "Oh, this guy who used to live on the ashram moved to Europe." Mr. Gold said, "He left the community."

I said, "Oh no, no, he's still a student. He just left the ashram." E.J. said to me again, "He left the community." I'm a slow learner, so I said, "No, no, he . . . " E.J. said, "He *left* the community."

Okay. Then Mr. Gold made a long, long teaching communication, which was that once you have reached a certain function within a spiritual school, within a Path, there is only one lawful direction in which you can move, which is toward the center. If you start to move away from the center, as far as Mr. Gold is concerned, you're gone. This particular student is still devoted to me, and he's involved in my trips to Europe, but according to Mr. Gold, that was a betrayal of the Work. In this particular kind of circumstance, he said it was being "guilty by virtue of fuck." That's a beautiful turn of a phrase, which really captures the essence of it.

Once we've gotten deeply into the Path, many of us are still very easily distracted, which is why the Indians call the mind "the monkey mind." You've got this great banana, but all of a sudden there's this apple over there. We are very easily distracted if there is even the slightest possibility that we might become famous or rich or satisfied sexually or healthy or whatever it is for each of us. My God, the amount of money that people spend just trying to stay healthy—the right supplements and vitamins and just the right massage—is sinful. Criminal! Eat clean food, exercise a little bit, do a little yoga, and stop stressing yourself with aggressive thoughts and behaviors, then you won't have to take all those supplements and vitamins. You will be fine.

Health, power, fame, whatever—we are easily distracted. We often aren't strong enough to apply a real sense of perspective and wisdom to the temptations that come our way. We are easily distracted and we don't have the wisdom to understand: "If I make this choice, this is the consequence, this is the price I'm going to have to pay." Instead we are on the pillow meditating: "Fame . . . here I am, on the pillow meditating, I'm going to be a yogi . . . fame . . ."

Students come to me and say, "I'd like to be in a relationship with such and such a person." I say, "Have you mentioned it to the person yet?" Then they get embarrassed:

"Well we've been sleeping together for three weeks." What are you asking me for? You want my blessings when you're already in the thing? Take responsibility for it. You need to ask me *before* you get involved, so if it's the worst combination of people imaginable, I can say no, wrong person. Don't ask me afterward!

With guru yoga you throw yourself at the mercy of the guru's instruction, and you follow that instruction. The process of life will reveal your entire inner landscape equally well. Instead of having this entire workshop full of tools and spiritual technology, all you have is your reliance on the guru. So you better have a lot of trust, because you may have to pass through a lot of unknown territory without a map.

I'll tell you another interesting story about Mr. Gold. He loves to use video games as a training ground for discipleship. He used these games that you play in teams, in which you develop skills and increase the number of weapons you can use until eventually you get powers like flying and invisibility and so on. They played "Zelda," a game in which you have to go through labyrinths and different castles to rescue the princess. In the process you meet killers and dragons and face the fire pit and all these things that are out there to stop you from getting the princess. You begin the game going through the first door into the first labyrinth with nothing but a candle. As you get through various labyrinths with the candle, then you get an axe and swords and a bow and arrow and then magic swords and so on.

As a way of developing skills for the Work, they would choose to play "Zelda" moving through the labyrinths with nothing but a candle—no swords or bows and arrows or magical tools. They would keep playing with nothing but the candle until they got to the end of the game and rescued the princess. It took a long time—maybe years—to develop that kind of proficiency. In fact, it was almost impossible. That's sort of like guru yoga. The guru is the candle, and that's all you have to rely on. You have to get through the entire labyrinth without relying on all of the fancy tools of the trade.

In Tibetan yoga there's a level of initiatory transmission where you learn to create this inner heat called *tummo*. The test for whether you've mastered the technology is to go up in the Himalayas—or in the Alps if you're a Swiss—and sit out there with no clothes on except a loincloth, because you don't want your sexual organs to freeze to the earth. Your teacher keeps throwing soaking wet blankets on you all night, which instantly freeze, and you have to melt the blanket. When you've passed the night melting each blanket that the teacher has thrown at you in sub-zero, freezing temperatures, then your teacher will know that you have mastered the technique of internal body heat and you go on to the next initiatory level in the labyrinth.

Suppose you're seriously studying shamanism. It's very helpful to be able to become a panther or an eagle; if you have to stay a man or a woman, things are a little tougher, because there are a lot of things an eagle can do that a man or a woman cannot do. If you're practicing guru yoga religiously you don't have any technology; it's just you, your intelligence, your body, your mind—that's it. No tools, no fancy yogas, no internal energy cycles, no nothing. Just you and your raw capacity, your raw ability. Wow, that's scary!

It's scary because once you start looking into your inner landscape, its not all light and love down there. We all have some pretty terrifying monsters in there. Not really, because the monsters are illusory, but they look real in the moment when they jump out of the dark and say, "Hi!" Their teeth are dripping with blood, and you know that you're going to be their next meal. Even though they are illusions, it's hard to know they're illusions in those moments. So, guru yoga is to move through every labyrinth without any of the fancy technology and nothing but trust in the guru.

They say Jesus died for our sins. I may be out of my area of expertise here, but what do you think that means? If you take it lawfully according to spiritual law, it means that there are no consequences to your sins because Jesus takes all the consequences. You go through your life happy as pigs in shit, doing whatever you want, incurring debt with unlimited credit cards, and Jesus pays. Think about it. If in fact Jesus died for your sins, then you are free and clear, innocent as a baby, and Jesus will be paying for eternity for your sins. That's why Christians say charity begins at home, and why you want to live a life of decency and good works. It's not for you; it's for Jesus, because Jesus is the Savior. You love the Savior, and you want to save Jesus a life of eternity in hell, so you do good works—but it's not for you, because you don't have any consequences. All the consequences of your shit go to Jesus. You get it? Most priests don't know that; they don't have a clue.

In any case, it's guru yoga or the path of heroic practice. The path of heroic practice is minimization—not necessarily renunciation, but minimization: pure diet, pure lifestyle, no jewelry, unadorned clothing. Heroic practice is a life of pure simplicity. Guru yoga is a path of radical reliance on the guru. Ultimately we come to the same end result, which is that we travel our inner landscape. We move through whatever labyrinths bring us to the roots of what makes us think and speak and move as we do, and we purify those roots. We replant the entire system.

ॐ

Guru Yoga

If you understand who the guru is, then surrender to the guru is surrender to the natural process of the Universe as it is unfolding. The guru is not just the person of the guru. If you are only surrendering to a person who you trust as a person, sooner or later—and probably sooner—that's going to be problematic. Of course there is the person of the guru, who will ask you to do things, and who you will have to obey as a way of paying your dues. That's why you need to choose the right guru. If you say, "I will obey you" to a teacher who is only interested in power, you will be taken advantage of and used up.

The first time I came to France my behavior was a little bit enigmatic. I had no students in France yet, so all the people who were coming to see me were either students of Arnaud Desjardins or Yvan Amar. While I was there everybody was panting with enthusiasm, but without my energy to obscure their concerns, some people were disturbed. Some of the things I was saying and doing had created doubt in the minds of some people. So, after I left for America, someone asked Arnaud in a public space, "Is Lee a true master?" Arnaud said, "I don't know anything about who is a true master and who is not a master. What I know something about is disciples, and I can say that Lee is a good disciple of his master."

I absolutely love that story! I think it's such an amazing, fabulous story that, without exaggeration, I've probably told it fifty times over the years, because I don't believe someone can be a really competent master unless they are a competent disciple first. When I am speaking about guru yoga, I am talking about a lineage and a tradition. The guru is never just a person; the guru is an entire history. In Tibetan Buddhism, which is over one thousand years old, when someone starts a formal ritual prayer they have to first offer gratitude to the entire lineage of gurus—one thousand years' worth—before they enter into the actual prayer. Even the greatest master, like the Karmapa, offers gratitude to the lineage. They start with the original, historical guru and go all the way up to the present, to the current living teacher; for everybody who was his student, the Karmapa's was the last name on the list.

So, when we engage guru yoga, we are getting the entire wisdom, force, experience, blessing and Benediction of the whole lineage. To me, that has relevance.

If someone goes on a vision quest in the mountains and has a little bit of insight into the nature of reality, then they say they are enlightened and start taking students—that's a tough one for me. I know a lot of those people. I like some of them; they're decent people. They just don't know what they're doing.

When I talk about guru yoga, I am referring to a whole universe of resource that gets drawn upon—absolutely not just one person's life experience and intelligence. I have a bias, because once I found my master, I was in forever. When I was in India with my master, every day, twice a day, He would ask me to give a talk to whoever was assembled in darshan. Sometimes it was whoever was traveling with me and three other people—all Indians, and none of them understood a word of English—and sometimes it was big crowds of thousands of people. I never spoke the way I do in the West; I never even said "damn" or "shit." Never. I spoke in refined language in the traditional way about practice and sadhana, and I never made off-color jokes.

My master didn't want a bunch of Western people running about in Europe and America looking like Indians. He was very clear with me and His Western disciples. Sometimes when Western tourists would come He would say to them, "Do you go to church? Do you love Jesus?" If they looked at Him like He was crazy, He would say, "Well, you're Christian aren't you? You're a Westerner. You're not Hindu—so, come on, what are you doing here?" I like to think that the only differences between my teaching and my master's teaching are qualities of culture and personality.

In the Baul tradition, which I am associated with, it is appropriate to have different gurus for specific functions. One of the hallmarks of the Baul tradition is the use of song, dance, sung poetry and choreography as a theatrical vehicle for the teaching, but every Baul guru is not necessarily capable of teaching those technical skills. For instance, the first guru is the master who teaches you music and poetry and movement but who is not your ultimate guru—your root guru.

For example, Ravi Shankar, the famous Indian sitar player, and Ali Akbar Khan, the drum player, both have music schools in America. If you want to learn from these two traditional music gurus, the first thing you have to do is sweep the floor, sometimes for years. You don't get to touch an instrument until you have proven to them—until they are satisfied—that you're going to enter into the teaching and stay with the teaching. When you are working with a guru, you need to have discipline. You need to be able to put up with tremendous humiliation; of course, it's not really humiliation, but to us it seems like humiliation.

One of the things that you can consider with guru yoga is that things are rarely black and white. Most things have fuzzy edges, in between somewhere. You want to be committed enough to learn and make progress but also strong enough and clear enough within yourself to be able to stop quickly and move quickly, if necessary. Like a tennis player or a martial artist, when something unexpected happens we need to be able to move quickly, right on the spot. That might mean following the teacher; that might mean not following the teacher. It could mean anything. You don't want to hold back out of neurosis or fear and miss what the teacher has to offer, and you want to have enough clarity within yourself to be able to instantly move one way or another, if necessary, because very few things are black and white.

On the other hand, sometimes a spiritual teacher will say to a student, "Alright, this lifetime is your chance. You've found your way here, and this is my last lifetime; I'm not going to be around anymore. It's now or never." I do not agree with that approach. My master made it clear—to other people who I heard it from, but never to me—that He and I had been together in past lifetimes in India. It's never "now or never." We come to this lifetime with a certain opportunity that we either take advantage of or not. If we don't take advantage of it now, we have another opportunity in some other lifetime, some other place, some other existence.

So when somebody says to you, "You have one chance, this is it," as a way of kind of getting us to move in a certain way, things are rarely that black or white. Maybe there is a certain potential in this moment that's not going to be there in the next moment because of the time and place and circumstance—okay, that's possible. Certainly, timing is everything; for anyone who has ever studied comedy, the first law of comedy is that timing is everything. There is some reality to understanding that certain times are better for some things, as long as we also understand that even the principle of timing has fuzzy edges. We want to stay away from cutting, hard-edged absolutes.

If somebody says to you, "There is only one way that I can teach you this certain thing—through sex," then that person is full of shit. Turn around and walk away, because they don't know what they're talking about. It is categorically untrue, always. Listen people, Jesus was monogamous—and I am not talking about God. I'm talking about Magdalene. If anybody could have transmitted the Christ light through sex, it would have been Jesus, and he didn't do it. He had one woman. There are many biblical scholars who agree that Jesus was married and had a child—you know, the Holy Grail is really the bloodline of Jesus. It might be true, and this is the popular contemporary viewpoint, but who knows? We'll never really know the truth.

At a certain time in Tibetan Buddhism, the use of sex as a shock technique for the transmission of certain states of consciousness was an accepted form of relationship with a committed disciple. Sex is not the same in Tibet as it is in the West, where you have all the flirtation and sentiment and romance in sex. In Tibet you have sex, and then you go work. You don't have sex and then lie around for hours caressing one another, saying sweet things and whispering words of love; you have sex and then you take care of the oxen. And remember, just because somebody was born in Tibet and is Tibetan by culture does not mean that they are a tulku or a rinpoche worthy of having sex with every Western woman who wants to be their disciple.

On the subject of guru yoga and surrender to the guru, I tend to discourage most people from becoming students of mine. There are times when someone asks to be a student and

I immediately say, "Yes, okay, no problem," but usually I discourage people. I tend to set up a labyrinth for people to find their way through before letting them in the door. Sometimes setting up the labyrinth just gets done for me, and I don't even know what's going on until afterward. People's trust is a great burden, because I have a certain personal integrity. When somebody gives me their trust, I want to do right by it. I'm neurotic and I have bad habits and I'm an asshole, so the fewer people who are around, the easier it is to bring integrity to their trust. If there were three, four or five hundred students, how could I possibly be able to respond to all of that trust?

So I make it difficult. Sometimes I insult people. Sometimes I insult someone *for* other people in the room, not for the poor person I insulted; the example doesn't matter because the principle is obvious. When it comes to guru yoga, it not only requires great trust on the part of the student, it also requires great trust on the part of the guru, because the guru has to act in a way that optimizes the student's progress.

Purna and I loved one another, but we struggled a lot. We had some pretty big fights, and at a certain point the struggle seemed to have just resolved for Purna. There wasn't any more fighting. Of course, when there was no more fight in him, there was no more fight in me, so it was a lovely situation. It was the exact, pivotal moment in which the opportunity, the door, opened for him to teach. He didn't want to teach. He had wanted to teach for fifteen years, and as soon as he didn't want to teach, it was time for him to teach.

For me, it was wonderful and terrible at the same time, because he goes out and makes mistakes, and I'm going to pay for those mistakes more than he is. That's the spiritual law. That's the way it works. I am shaking in my boots! "Oh my God! What disasters is this guy going to get himself into?"

Purna and I are very different—not essentially, but in personality—meaning, what trouble is he going to get me in? But I knew it was the right moment. It was very clear, and I had to trust him the same way he had to trust me. He was very solid about it. He was really *there*. It wasn't like he was just doing something that was spiritually correct. I had to sort of push him a little and really support him because he was also a little bit tentative. Both of us were. So, it's really a situation of mutual trust; it's not a one-way street.

The relationship with the guru is reciprocal. In the same way, we could say that the Work feeds us and we feed the Work; it's a reciprocal process. In Buddhism, they give special merit to the mother of the Buddha; who's to say that we aren't one of the mothers or fathers of the Buddha? Let's take the poetry of Baudelaire as an example: people who love his poetry probably never think of the woman or women who inspired that poetry. His poetry communicates a certain kind of tragic love, but it is a big love, and it's entirely possible that the woman who inspired that poetry, in the eyes of the Work, is just as important as Baudelaire.

God has a cosmic interview, but we see two percent of the perspective. God sees three hundred and sixty degrees. In the Army there is usually a point man who goes out ahead of the rest of the troup to see if the territory they are moving into is safe. Nobody wants to be the point man, because if there is a land mine, guess who steps into it first? The point man is the one who takes the brunt of the attention. If there's a sniper in the bushes, guess who gets hit? Like with Baudelaire, the artist gets most of the worldly attention while the source of the inspiration gets very little, but to the Work, to the Path, they may get equal attention or even more attention.

In this process of guru yoga, every one of us feeds the Work in a different way, and somebody has to wash the dishes and fix the cars. We often draw the unconscious conclusion that the hardest worker and the person in front are getting the most blessings. People visit our ashrams and think that the people living on the ashram must be the best students because they are with me all the time. Not necessarily. One of my students died last year; I wish everyone could have a death like that because he died consumed with devotion to his guru—to Yogi Ramsuratkumar and to me. He died very well. People who weren't around the brilliance of his death probably have no idea of how well he died, because he had that kind of practice—he was invisible. He never created art, he never traveled with me, but he died really well, and you get a lot of points for that.

Each one of us has our own unique, personal relationship to the guru and to the Work. Some of us get a lot of external attention—we are out in front—but to the eyes of the Work, people in the background are every bit as evident. We want to be very careful not to diminish ourselves in our own minds because we don't have a "glory position." You do not want to be putting obstacles between your teacher and yourself by criticizing yourself; how would we know whether we have anything to offer the Work? When someone has a lot of self-hatred psychologically speaking, it is hard to convince them of their value to the Work. When someone feels unattractive on any level, it's hard to convince them that they actually are attractive.

One of my students is a fifth degree black belt in aikido, and he once started a seminar he gave by saying, "Lee keeps saying I'm a fifth degree black belt, but there are thousands of them in the world—it's not a big deal." For him, the value of the practice of aikido is not in the title. One of the rarest qualities on the Path is true humility. A lot of people look humble, but it's just their self-hatred. We want to be able to realize these principles within ourselves and understand that the Work responds to qualities within that are not necessarily qualities that are used to define "success" in the external world. In the external world we value a certain physical vivacity, but the Work has a whole different criteria.

In the gross world we are impressed by the appearance of things. In the outer world, except in our area of expertise, we tend to be impressed by the appearance of things—like theatre productions. Most theatre is good, but there is a difference between outstanding theatre and good theatre. Al Pacino took a radical production of a Shakespeare play off Broadway and the critics just slaughtered the piece because they were looking at the radical portrayal of Shakespeare rather than the brilliance that Pacino brought to it.

We tend to misunderstand the guru, the Path and the Work. We tend to think that the guru judges us by the criteria that the world judges by. Students are always coming to me and crying about this, that and the other thing, and none of it means anything to me at all! E.J. Gold says that everybody thinks they have some fantastic talent to offer the Work, but often that is the very last thing the Work wants from us. We assume that the guru's value system is identical to our psychological bias. We do not want to diminish our sense of our own value—or our faith in the Path and the guru—because we are not the best looking or the hardest worker. It is not people's external skills that necessarily attract me to them as a student. In fact, I much prefer it when my students are ugly and unattractive, because then I don't have to worry about being distracted and becoming "star struck"!

I can spot potential in a student, and my only interest is in what serves the Work. I have a very good sense of what someone's value to the Path is. For some of my students who are writers or artists, they are serving the Path with their art, but those skills are not their essential value. Even if they didn't have those skills, they would still be just as useful to the Work as they are with those skills. For others, the only value they have to the Work is their art. Obviously, in the sangha there will be all kinds of situations for people: some people will participate and some won't; some will make very big contributions and others will be invisible. Do not presume to have the wisdom of the Path. When you judge others, you do them a great disservice, because you are judging them through the veil of your own psychology, not through the wisdom of the Work. When you are judging someone in the sangha, you are presuming to have the viewpoint of the Work, and there is only one way to get qualified to make that presumption: if your guru qualifies you.

I am very critical of my students on a verbal level. I am always using my students, generally speaking, as examples. I don't name names, but I say, "Oh my students, they're nothing but worms and frogs and they can't do shit!" And, "How in the hell did I ever end up with this bunch of losers?" Things like that. They are the sacrifices for my teaching examples, whether my criticisms are true or not. There's this joke they used to tell when I was in high school: What's French foreplay, Italian foreplay and Jewish foreplay? I don't remember any of them except Italian foreplay. What's Italian foreplay? Turn over! In other words: No foreplay! They say in the business world, time is money. You don't make any profit kissing and caressing for an hour and a half. Let's make the deal and go on to the next deal! Fifteen minutes, that was nice. Go make me breakfast. I wish I could say all that in a romantic context, but . . .

As long as you are welcomed by the guru, take it. Do not judge it, do not try to figure it out. If all you do is hang around, enjoy the vacation, because it won't last forever. Sooner or later, in this relationship of guru yoga, the Work is going to come to you, and when the Work comes to you, you are going to work.

So, have a nice evening. If anything I've said has disturbed you, go out dancing tonight. I'm serious—have a good dinner, go out dancing, hear some good music. You'll completely forget about everything. That's the cure for most everything. If anything I said is getting you to consider Reality, go dancing tonight. Take my advice. What a dream! It's a dream, but oh, it's a wonderful dream. It's one of those dreams you wake up from and say, "Oh, that was great." You jump out of bed, and you're full of energy. So, if you need to, go dancing tonight. Don't get up tomorrow saying, "I couldn't sleep last night, something you said yesterday really, really got to me." Forget it. Go dancing.

And if you're feeling great—you're feeling so good that you're practically floating on air, you're almost in ecstasy, you could practically trip leaving the room—then cheese and meat for you tonight! Lots of cheese and lots of meat. Don't worry, you won't feel light anymore.

ॐ

The Work Is Not the Adversary

The Work is about profit for the Work, but profit for the Work means profit for you. Energy for the Work means energy for you—you're not separate from that. When Teresa of Avila took vows and became a nun, she didn't stop being a creative, vivacious, lively, happy, brilliant woman. In fact she was always making trouble in the convent because she loved practical jokes, and she was full of life, laughing and loud and social. Sometimes the Mother Superior didn't like that. Luckily her confessor was John of the Cross, and they shared a perfect resonance relative to their devotion to God. So everything worked out very nicely. If you read their poetry, you'd think that they talked about poetry a lot together.

If you take care of the Work, the Work is going to take care of you. It's not going to crush you and wipe out your personality. It's really important to understand that. The Work is not the enemy, because sometimes we actually think that way. We literally act as if the guru is our enemy, our adversary. "Oh, I love the guru and I'm devoted to the Path, but it's just so hard, so demanding, so devouring, so total." We act as if the guru is the enemy and the Path is our adversary, like we have to defend ourselves against our guru. When they're being honest with themselves, some of my students will say,

"If I don't defend myself a little bit against Lee, he's just going to use me up."

When you are working with your own psyches, your own minds, you really want to take the position that the Work is not your adversary and the guru is not your enemy. "I do not need to defend myself against the intrusion of God, who wants to take my soul and use me up." The greatest joy of some of my students who are musicians is composing music. If I give them ten songs to compose and they have to stay up all night composing those songs, they're going to be ecstatic by the time the morning comes. They're not going to be like, "Fucking Lee, I couldn't sleep all night. Bastard! Why does he do this to me?"

It's not like that. I will ask people for things, and what I ask people for are the things that will most profit those people. One of my students has had a lifelong hate/love relationship with her father—mostly hate. She wanted to have nothing to do with her father, but there was some love there, so she said to me, "I'm supposed to go visit my father. It's a family anniversary, and everybody comes to it at the same time every year. I haven't been there in years. I can't be in the same room with the guy without getting angry."

I said to her, "Never mind *you*. Your father wants to see you. No matter how much of a bastard he is, you're his daughter and he loves you in some way. Go just for a weekend, not for a whole week. Go for a weekend and just serve the guy. Forget yourself and all your emotions and just go for him." The first time she visited him, she struggled somewhat, but she did it. Then the next year when they had the family party, she went back again, and she brought her grown daughter who her father had seen only a couple of times in his life. She kept going back and over four or five years there has been a major healing in the whole family. She said, "Oh, I never thought it could be like this." It was obvious to me.

The main thing is a complete freeing up of energy. There was a veil. There were chains on her that had completely freed up. When the guru makes recommendations to people, he has no investment in people's happiness and success. He wants their happiness and success for them. A real teacher stands free. He can take care of himself; he doesn't need other people's successes to reflect on him. When he makes recommendations, it's purely for the person he is making the recommendations for.

We really do not want to get into the habit of unconsciously viewing the Path, the guru, the school, as in some way being dangerous or adversarial to us. We do not want to get into that habit, but that habit can develop little by little by little, until all of a sudden there it is. So you want to stop it instantly, as soon as it raises its head, because if you don't cut off its head the instant it appears, before you know it you've got a seven-headed dragon, and you are not going to get all those heads off. You've got to handle it in a different way. Okay, maybe even two heads, but seven? Metaphorically speaking, what do you do if you find a dragon with seven heads? Forget its heads—cut its nuts off! You're not going to get all those seven heads off without at least one of those heads making serious inroads into your health. If there's only one head it's easy—you just keep cutting the head off. It will keep re-growing, but you just keep cutting the head off, no problem.

We have a certain idea of what success is. Sometimes we develop this very bizarre idea that if we really surrender to the Work our lives are going to fall apart, our relationships are going to fall apart, our businesses are going to fall apart, and we're not going to be able to create art. I don't know where that idea came from, but it's a ridiculous, unnecessary, stupid idea. Listen, if your primary relationships are based on lies, yes, the Work is going to bring you a little bit of a reality check. You bet. If in your business you are a lying, thieving, manipulating businessman, the Work is going to bring a few lessons to your approach. But essentially the Influence of the Work will strengthen your relationships and bring you more material success and a greater capacity to create art. Not less, more. Why not?

One of the things that the guru does is protect us. The guru's Influence—Divine Influence—is not a guarantee that we'll always be healthy and successful and we'll never lose our favorite piece of jewelry or our wallet. However, the guru protects us. After I met Yogi Ramsuratkumar, I understood to some degree the pervasiveness of His Influence in my life—even in my early life, before I found the Path. I realized that He protected me in many ways from very serious physical and social problems.

Before I got into the Work I was in the rare stamps and coins business, where there were a lot of people whose ethics were quite questionable. I had the opportunity to be in partnership with some of those people to varying degrees. They were charismatic and eloquent in their speech, and they were really able to build up the dream. I never got into partnership with those people, and it saved me money and integrity and maybe even kept me out of jail. Somehow the people I actually got into partnership with were honest and reliable.

There was a very intimate network that we worked in, and everybody knew that one of the guys was sort of questionable, but we did business with him because there was lots of money and opportunity, and it was very useful. At one point the word went out on the street that this guy had been taken in by the FBI. His phone had been tapped, so everybody who called his business phone for a week got their phone number recorded by the FBI. Panic went into the business, "Oh my

God!" The only person who ended up going to jail was that guy, but we were all really scared for a while. We thought that we were looking at some big problems in our lives!

When I was nineteen I wanted to be rich and famous. It was really a very stupid thing, because my parents were generous, and I never wanted for anything. I was very well cared for; I didn't have to struggle. I always had the toys I wanted and the bicycle I wanted. Thank God those were the days before video games! I had my erector set. Then when I went to university, I came back for my first Christmas vacation and there was a brand-new car sitting in my parents' driveway. I never wanted for anything, but somehow, even though it was a stupid thing, I wanted to be rich and famous.

I started my own business when I was twenty years old, back in 1964. I was in the business of selling silver and gold coins, which is why I still love silver and gold so much. I was twenty years old and my partner was seventeen, and a special coin came out in America: the first silver fifty-cent piece with a picture of John Kennedy on the front. Some coin dealer said to us, "These things are selling in Italy for twenty dollars apiece," and it was a fifty-cent piece. He said, "I can get bags of a thousand of these things—a thousand dollars' worth. I'll give you guys the bags, because you're young and innocent and you just look like college kids. It's illegal, but nobody will ever find out—you get on an airplane, you take these things to Italy. I'll arrange somebody to buy them, and we'll split the money." We said to each other, "If we each take one bag of these things, we're going to make twenty thousand dollars apiece." We were just kids; if we went to a convention and made five hundred dollars over a week, we were jumping for joy. Twenty thousand dollars! We were very enthusiastic, but we didn't do it, because we would have been arrested in Italy and thrown in jail. I'd be getting out just about now!

I can see that I was really protected by Yogi Ramsuratkumar. I was a very impulsive, naïve young man, and I would have done things that would have been extremely dangerous. Somehow, just when you're ready to do something that could be dangerous, you get a little distracted, and somehow you aren't able to do it. Really, you are saved. I knew lots of people who were in Vietnam, especially in the years when I was teaching the Silva Method. There were a lot of people coming back who had seen incredible violence on the front lines, and they were scarred. I was saved from that. I got drafted, and I was just going to go along with it, but my mother stepped in and said, "They're not taking you." I would have gone where they sent me—I had no protest within me—but my mom confronted the U.S. government and got an exemption for me. Even my mother worked for Yogi Ramsuratkumar!

So, the guru protects you, which is one of the other benefits of guru yoga, but it's important to understand that what gets protected is our work, not necessarily our emotional sensitivities. It doesn't mean that nothing in our lives will create grief or pain for us because we have surrendered to the guru. Many of my students are getting to the age where a lot of their parents, if they haven't died already, are going to die soon. They're in their late eighties or nineties, and it's time for them to go. Many of them have been sick for years and are really suffering in uncomfortable circumstances, but even so we hold on. Our intelligence says, "Yes, they've led a good life and they're old and things are deteriorating; it's time for them to go," but our emotions are just holding on. The Influence of the guru doesn't necessarily protect our emotionality when we are off—it protects our work. If it is to the benefit of your work for your mother or father to live a bit longer, then that's what gets blessed. If it's a benefit to your work for your parent to die sooner, that's what happens.

One of the things that most people deal with relative to money is the dichotomy between their outer level of relationship and their inner level of relationship. On the outside most of us have a relatively positive attitude. We'd like to have enough money to satisfy our basic needs, maybe to travel, to indulge once in a while in something fancy, some nice art, or to not have to compromise when it comes to our children and their needs. But internally . . . ? As I've already said, there are laws to our relationship to money. Someone once said that the only armor God can't pierce is the ego. It's our responsibility to open the gates of ego so that God can come in, because if we keep the gates closed, God can set up a siege, close off the source of food and everything, but ego is like a medieval city: inside there are gardens that grow food and a well with water and everything else we think we need.

So, the obvious question is: How do we open the gates of ego? It's our responsibility to get to the roots of our worldview. We can't attack the kingdom of heaven; we have to open the doors of ego so the Divine can raise us. There is an elevator to heaven, but unfortunately the doors to the elevator are the doors to ego. One of the things we have to do is be willing to suffer any amount of being revealed exactly as we are. Most of us aren't willing to be revealed. If we really stop to think about it, the things we are afraid of other people knowing about us are ridiculous little things—they're not important things.

There was a woman in the community who left very morally uptight and righteous. I used to look at her and think, "God, what kind of an upbringing did this poor thing have?" She was a very pretty little thing, so I was always gentle with her and very solicitous. I felt a little sorry for her boyfriend, but it was okay. Then we had this thing in the community we call men's culture and women's culture: the men get together and hash out their problems with other men so they don't burden their partners, and the women get together with other women and hash their problems out. The men get together, "You got any problems?" No. "You got any problems?" No. And the women talk and talk. It's works out really great! So, because of the women's group, I happened to find out that this morally uptight, ethically righteous little thing was a major cocaine user at university, had had five abortions . . . Geez! Part of her external personality was trying to hide her embarrassment about all that. So what if you took drugs—you're not taking them now!

When people come to the community, I say, "Don't tell me what you've done in the past." Some of the men who come here are really tough guys. Maybe these guys have killed people—I don't want to know! I come to meditation every morning, sit there and close my eyes; if I know there are two guys sitting on the men's side of the room who have killed people, I'm not going to be able to close my eyes. I just say, "Are you reformed?" Yes. "Fine!" I'm serious—but a different kind of serious.

We defend ourselves against what doesn't need defense. If you fall in love with somebody, and you find out that ten years ago they were addicted to heroin but now they're clean and they're good to you, they're generous—what difference does it make? If it does make a difference, it's your problem. Relax. When we fall in love with somebody, whoever they are, they've been around. It's very graceful when they don't tell us where they've been, but we know they've been around—if not this lifetime, then last lifetime. They're not the same person now, but there's some thread of connection there.

If we want to open the doors of ego, we have to relax. We have to understand that really for the most part, what we are defended against doesn't need to be defended against. If we did not defend certain things that we are embarrassed about in our past, nobody would know anyway. We don't have to defend ourselves, and if we don't tell anybody about those things, nobody's going to know about them. Anyone who has done any kind of bodywork knows that the longer we are defended, the more that defense effects the musculature and glandular balance in our bodies.

Of course, I'm totally defended. I like being defended. It's part of my charm. My women students say, "He's so defended, but it's so adorable." I'm not being very outrageous so far this week, but I tell people when I'm being outrageous, "I'm not really like this." I'm a completely defended, armored character. I've been complaining recently that nobody understands me. Well, why do I think nobody understands me? Because I completely mask who I am.

A teacher was invited to meet me for dinner the other night. He said to me, "What are you like?" I said, "I'm really shy." He said, "Oh sure! No you aren't." I said, "Yes, I'm really shy, I really am." He said, "You're joking," and I said, "No, I really am." Everything you see when I'm in front of the room talking is style. It's taken me thirty years to develop it. It's all an act. The performance is all an act, but what comes through is real.

We have to be willing to open the doors of ego, to relax our self-defense. I'm not talking about being stupid. I'm talking relaxing the self-defense relative to our fantasies and our imagination about what other people think of us, or what other people would think of us if they saw who we really were, underneath the veneer of our social charm and our moral uprightness and our political correctness—or whatever it is.

One of the books that I recommend is a particular translation of the Indian scripture, the *Bhagavata Purana,* Book Ten, which is about Krishna. There was a religious sect in the fifteenth century who had a guru named Sri Vallabhacharya, and he commented on these six chapters of scripture.

He taught that everything in the world has been created by Krishna to be enjoyed by Krishna's worshippers. So why not enjoy beautiful environments, comfortable circumstances, good food, deep and loving relationships? They're all gifts of Krishna, so take them. Sri Vallabhacharya's path was called "the pushti path"—the path of opulence and enjoyment. He and his followers were completely against the extreme, ascetic renunciation of many Indian paths. That's why Krishna as a young man is shown with a woman, Radha or one of the gopis, on his arm. That image doesn't just represent sex; it represents the interaction of the masculine and the feminine—the feminine being the material world, and in particular those things that are fine, rich, beautiful and juicy. It's not about being some skinny yogi on top of a mountain, meditating twelve hours a day.

We often have this idea that things are going to fall apart if we get a little too close to the heart of the Work. It's true that we are going to see more clearly, but that often gives us the wisdom and the capacity to actually repair the tears in our lives that are straining the material. Those tears by themselves—unrepaired—would destroy everything. If you enter into the Work and you're starting to see things more clearly, and in that seeing clearly and in the instruction that you are realizing is valuable instruction, you are completely bullheaded and completely insensitive and unwilling to respond softly and to meet the demand of life halfway—if you are completely stubborn and angry and abusive—of course the Work is going to create some discomfort in your life. That's not the fault of the Work.

One of the things I like to do in Arizona when guests come is to have a fine meal to honor the guest. If I want a fine meal cooked, the people I'm going to ask to cook it are the people who are in a good mood, who are enthusiastic, who are grateful to have the opportunity, and who have some skill in the kitchen. It's common sense. I'm not going to ask somebody who is angry and feeling taken advantage of, because the quality of the food and the mood of the environment is going to be different depending upon who's in the kitchen cooking.

The Work wants you to be able to serve God. That's the bottom line. God wants to be served, but who is going to serve God best? Someone who is happy and healthy and feeling full of confidence and enthusiasm, or someone who's broke and feeling betrayed and abandoned? If you meet the Work—not even halfway, just a little bit—then the Work is going to shower you with positive blessings, because the Work wants you to be in a state of mind in which you're grateful and enthusiastic and willing to serve. The Work is not going to crush you just because the Work has the power and authority to crush you. What a ridiculous viewpoint.

ॐ

You're the Scary Ones

There's this interesting phenomena: sometimes people tend to be afraid of me. They have these reactions, as if I'm some kind of scary guy. People will say, "Oh, I'm scared of your teaching, it's so tough." Or, "I'm sacred of you, you're so fierce!" Let me explain what the problem is: You're the scary ones. What is inside of you that is afraid of me is the thing that's really scary. So when anyone is having a reaction to me, it's a reaction to your own internal underworld. It the catastrophe that is your ego, attempting not to be what it is, self-centeredly, that is scary—*really* scary.

In some of the traditions they say that the guru is a mirror: when you look at the guru, you see yourself. I have never really emphasized that position. I think that's a good excuse for avoiding yourself—a good reason to maintain superficiality. "The guru is a mirror, the guru is a mirror," is a mantra that is equal in power to, "Coca-Cola, Coca-Cola."

There is something very scary about having to take an entire lifetime—in spite of the fact that the lifetime is neurotic, and maybe even psychotic—and begin to live it differently. That's very scary. It's as scary as the first time you visit a country that is very foreign to your own country. The first time we visited India in 1976 there were six of us: four men and two women. We arrived exhausted, very late at night, found a hotel somewhere and went right to sleep.

When we got up in the morning, I said, "Let's go out on the streets and get some atmosphere, absorb some culture!" We walked out on the street, and it turned out that we had found a hotel in an area that was not a tourist area. Many of the people there had literally never seen a Westerner. Immediately we were surrounded by about fifty people—they weren't violent or loud, they were just curious. The women traveling with me were very afraid, because nothing like this would ever happen in the West, unless it was riot or people were going to tear you apart and eat you or something. Both of the women on that trip learned to love India and traveled there many times—they learned to relax once they had some understanding—but the first response was fear, because it was so *radically* different.

The same is true of our psychology: the way things are is comfortable, even if we have bad habits. Even if we're full of self-hatred and self-destructive behavior, we're used it, so it's very scary to consider entering into a territory that is completely foreign to us. But the thing that is useful to understand is that in our ordinary life structures, absolutely nothing will change. If you're in a profession that you hate, or you're in a relationship that's completely untenable, *maybe* those things will change, but that would happen anyway under ordinary circumstances.

In the Work, the only thing that changes is the way we see things. The actual content of our lives—why would it change? We have our homes, we have our families, we have our friends, we have the kind of music we like and the kind of movies we like—why would any of that change? In essence, what we're afraid of is an illusion. We have this idea, this projection: "Oh, if I surrender to God, I'll be thrown in a meat grinder and ripped to pieces." Really, that's the kind of projection we have.

Let's use Saint Francis and Saint Claire as examples: How many young Catholic men and women were there in that part of the country? Thousands, tens of thousands? And how many Saint Francises and Saint Claire were there? A handful? Think about it. When I'm teaching I tend to use very dramatic examples: Milarepa or Naropa or other fantastic Tibetan Buddhists, Saint Teresa of Avila or Saint Francis, or even Jesus for that matter. If you study the historical records of the time of Jesus, there were *hundreds* of people who claimed to be the Messiah. Most of them were just first century psychotherapists! There was only one Jesus. Those are all dramatic examples, but they serve as a catalyst, an inspiration, upon which we stand. The dramatic example is not meant to indicate that every one of us, if we really practice hard, will become such a dramatic example.

Yogi Ramsuratkumar was married. He had three children, and He was the principal—the headmaster—of a school for children. He was ripped out of His circumstance by a kind of divine obsession; He left His family and profession and went wandering on the road, but He did not recommend that to His disciples. He did not recommend that they take on a renunciate lifestyle; in fact, He was tremendously solicitous to families. He recommended that Indian men treat their wives with honor and respect and decency—practically unheard of in Indian society.

Alcoholism is becoming a *very* serious social problem in India, but because it's mostly with the poor, you don't hear about it, it gets covered up. Who cares about the untouchables and the tribals? Let them all drink themselves to death and beat their wives—who cares? So, you don't hear about it, but it's a very, very big problem in India. Yogi Ramsuratkumar recommends that people stay in their families, take care of their families, work and be responsible. He doesn't recommend that they follow Him literally and do what He did.

We tend to have this unconscious projection about being annihilated. In the Sufi tradition they talk about "annihilation" and "ruin"—we think, "Oooh, that's ugly!" They don't mean that your life falls to pieces and you become completely irresponsible, or that you end up on the streets covered with every kind of sore from every kind of horrible disease, starving to death! In the Sufi tradition "ruin" means that your attention on anything besides God becomes improbable. What does it mean that your attention on anything besides God is improbable? It means that when you look at your husband or wife or children, instead of seeing them through your neurotic life script, you see them as they are, in the perfection of their natural essence. Should that be a problem? Is that something to be afraid of? Obviously not. What we fear is completely our projection, our expectation, our confusion, our misunderstanding. In fact, if we find ruin, we're actually more likely to have a stable family environment and a responsible position in the world—to be healthy and happy. *More* likely, not less likely.

I know there are many fine artists in this room. If we find ruin, our art becomes a genuine offering of sanctity to the world; in no way is it defined by our own need to feel self-worth because we're giving something to the world—or whatever our neurotic motive for creating art is. One of the things that makes a difference between a *technically* fine piece of art and something that *really* speaks to people is the clarity—or we could say the divinity—of the what-is-as-it-isness in the piece of art.

As we deepen our practice, we tend to hit certain moods in which there is a lot of concern, fear, confusion, doubt or whatever it might be. Those things are not based on an objective insight into reality; they are based on an illusion. I mean, I'm not scary. I get up here and I talk about sex, or say some tough things, but look at my life. Do I ever act that scary? Never! I'm a nerd, a wimp, a coward, a wuss! I'm maybe the least scary spiritual master in the West.

What we're afraid of is our own minds. We say, "You have to surrender to God! You have to give up all your attachments! You have to sacrifice everything!" But that's a statement of the distinction between seeing everything as separate and seeing everything as not separate. That's the distinction between accepting what is as it is here and now, and *not* accepting what is as it is here and now. Maybe we could even say it's a distinction between being clear-eyed and perceptive, and confused and in denial.

There is absolutely nothing to be afraid of. Many people unconsciously feel fulfilled when they feel that they're being victimized. "Oh my husband's a bastard and he doesn't understand me. All he cares about is business, he's never home, he has no time for his family." We complain about that, and we suffer it, but also at some deep subconscious level, it's very fulfilling because we're a victim in the circumstance and we get so much satisfaction from acting out our feelings of victimization. Suppose that simply by changing your viewpoint you could see how much pain your husband was in, and it was his *pain* that was creating his workaholism, or his fear of the innocence of his own children, or whatever. You might see that your husband—or your wife—was completely defined by a certain cultural expectation, and there was no consciousness involved. The inference is that you would have to take more personal responsibility for your own life and your position in that life.

A lot of my students are always saying to me, "I'm feeling this, that and the other thing, and I think I need therapy. What do you think?" In maybe one out of ten cases, I'll say,

"Yes, I think it's a good idea. Let's figure out what is the most viable form of therapy that would serve you," but in most cases I say, "You don't need therapy. What you need is the ability to make a clear distinction. You need to stand up for yourself and be able to say yes and no instead of being the victim of everything in life."

When we come to one of these periods in our practice where all of a sudden we're afraid, and we start saying to ourselves, "What if the teacher is going to take advantage of me? What if the teacher is going to hurt me? The teacher is a scary person," then we need to look at what it is we're actually afraid of *in ourselves*. In some way, shape or form, we're afraid of loss, but we have to define it more specifically: what are we afraid of losing? Maybe we're afraid of going mad. It's a very common fear—the ultimate loss of control.

Once as a teenager I was taking a bus somewhere, and there was a woman standing at the bus with a very scarred face. Everybody was staring at her—really *staring*, not being kind of discrete, but really staring at her. She was transfigured to the extent that it was shocking. Then she just broke and started screaming hysterically at the top of her lungs, "I can't take it anymore! I can't take it!" I was thirteen years old, and I had never seen anything like that before.

My mother and father did not scream. When my mother got pregnant, my mother and father stopped smoking and stopped drinking. Their only poison was black coffee, no sugar. So I grew up with no reference point for cigarettes, or drinking a little too much—I had no reference for it at all, or for any addictive habits at all.

When I was teaching the Silva Method, there was a woman in one of my classes. She took the course, and then she went home and practiced the methods. She called me up one day and said, "I have a problem." I said, "Well, come down, and we'll talk about it." I didn't know it at the time, but the problem was that she was having a nervous breakdown—she was in an extended psychotic break. She was very sane and intelligent on the phone, but when she came down, she was completely in some other reality. She was thinking that every metal screw and nail in the furniture was a receiving microphone for aliens, and I had no reference point for what she was going through. She was out there! She was completely out of control, and it was a very scary thing for me. Everything got handled fine, but it was scary.

I have a tremendous amount of awe and respect for people who work in psychiatric situations because those situations scare me. I have a couple of students who are psychiatric nurses, and it is hard work. You have to be really dedicated to do work like that.

All of our fears, in some way, shape or form, are about loss. A very common fear is: I'm going to go crazy. What if I go crazy? We look at Yogi Ramsuratkumar's circumstance and say, "Oh my God!" because He was divinely mad for a period of time. One great story of His divine madness is that He went into an ecstatic trance with His foot on a train track, and the train came along and took off part of His toes. While the train was running over His toe, in His mind the Divine was saying, "This is what happens to people who worship Ram." We hear that and say, "I'm not saying that mantra ever again!"

The experience of madness happened to Yogi Ramsuratkumar, but it was His task, it was His *job*, to be Yogi Ramsuratkuamr—a vehicle for a certain transmission of Grace. That is not all of our jobs. Swami Prajnanpad had a certain function, which is the function of his students necessarily. The function of Arnaud's students is not to do what he does, but perhaps to be who he is in reality, in essence, in truth. Sometimes when we read spiritual literature we get confused about a certain function that the guru has. Often we read some dramatic example, and something inside us will say, "Oh no, I'm not going there!" Sure, *every* once in a while—I mean very rarely—somebody will be in a state of disorientation, which we call ecstasy. We call it *ecstacy* because we're out of our usual state. Ordinarily when those things happen, which is rarely, they happen in a circumstance in which we're cared for, which is grace-full.

So mostly what we're afraid of is our own projection, which has nothing to do with reality. If we surrendered completely to God in this moment and gave our lives up, in the next moment we would still be sitting here going about the schedule of the day. For most of us the *only* difference—and there would be a difference—would be the way we saw all things: people and relationships and world situations and trees and animals and everything. We would be seeing things *as they are*, not as we imagined them to be. That would be the only difference.

For most of us, we aren't seeing trees; we're seeing our mental idea of that thing as a tree. Now that might seem like a very minor distinction; it might seem completely impractical to you: "What are we going to do with that?" From this side of the view, it's nothing but philosophy. It's completely useless as a piece of information. But if you take the testimonies of individuals in every tradition—Christian, Jewish, Buddhist, Hindu, shamanistic, animistic, Taoist, whatever—who have actually seen a tree *as it is*, they say there is a difference. So who are we to say? Nobody. Who are they to say? Somebody. Or the other way around, if you deep thinkers prefer!

That would be the only difference—we would see what is, as it is, here and now, exactly. The actual content of our lives, in the vast majority of cases, would not change at all, except on the relational level. Our families wouldn't change, our jobs wouldn't change, our houses wouldn't change, our cars wouldn't change, our tastes in clothing wouldn't change—well, maybe sometimes that would! But the difference in *how* we saw things would radically alter our entire view of reality, of life, of the Universe, in a positive way. So, in reality, there is nothing to be afraid of.

Rhetorically speaking, the nondualists say that as we are now, we are experiencing something, and when you make the shift, the difference is that experience simply arises. There is no "you"—separate from everything else—to experience what is arising. So to me, the Path is very clear. The question is: Within myself, would I rather have somebody to experience and suffer, or nobody to experience and not suffer in that way? To me, the answer is obvious; there is *no* question. I would rather have nobody to experience and no suffering. Most of us do not choose that answer; we chose the answer of, "I'm willing to suffer, because I want to be here; I don't want to disappear." We don't know what "I" disappearing is. So the choices we make are completely based on projection, expectation, illusion and confusion.

I use Arnaud Desjardins as an example and not myself because I'm cranky and easily driven to anger and reaction. Look at Arnaud: Is he somebody who has been driven mad and *destroyed*, *annihilated*, by having realized? He's a man of rich qualities, of a full life, active, interested in things, intelligent—so what's the problem? That's what you have to look forward to. The price you pay for surrender is to be like Arnaud. "Arnaud" is the gift you get! You're not going to be some skinny yogi with ugly hair and rotten teeth and big scabs on his ass like Milarepa. That's not who you get to be. When you shift, you get to be somebody who can experience life as it is, in all its fullness and beauty and ugliness and pain and sorrow and joy and delight and wonder. That's who you get to be! Not somebody who has lost everything, who is mad and out wandering the streets.

Yes, you still have to deal with reality. You still have to deal with the air pollution in the city, you still have to deal with the traffic, you still have to deal with brothers and sisters and aunts and uncles and mothers and fathers and lovers who may sometimes be problematical. Yes, you still have to deal with all of that. That's just life. It's not a problem; it's just life. Would you rather deal with those things straight ahead, clear-eyed, full of life, or would you rather deal with those things from a position of feeling like you're a victim, full of self-hatred and fear? You deal with those things just as they are, straight on.

I saw Yogi Ramsuratkumar two weeks a year when He was alive. The rest of the time, I couldn't just call Him up. He wasn't like me—you couldn't just write a letter or call Him up and get an answer to your question. He didn't answer. When I asked Yogi Ramsuratkumar questions, if I ever did, He would just laugh. "Oh, thanks for the answer. What does that mean?" Then He'd laugh harder.

I have these responsibilities to students. Many years ago we lived in New Jersey, and it was getting more and more violent. There was a rape in the parking lot of the mall where we always went shopping, and everybody was getting scared. We had to move somewhere, so I said, "Okay, we've got to get out of here. Let's move to the country, to Arizona." I couldn't call up Yogi Ramsuratkumar and say, "What should I do?" Life just provides opportunities—all you have to do is have a tiny little bit of sensitivity. Just keep your eyes open, and life gives you all you need.

Yogi Ramsuratkumar's Influence organizes my life. That's why you want to be in a tradition, in a lineage. I don't hear voices or have dreams where He comes and says, "Do this."

Some people do—not me. He just organizes things so that, like a good rat in a good maze, I just go right along. Personally I love it that way. Life is big and overwhelming—I don't want to make my own choices. I want my master to set everything up so nicely and smoothly that I just flow down the river.

We go to California, Los Angeles, New York City or Mexico City and see that people spend four to six hours every day in their cars, going to work and coming home from work. I say to myself, how can anyone live that way? Why don't they move? Okay, maybe if they moved they wouldn't make as much money or they'd have to be more creative, but my God, four, five, six hours a day, to and from work, five days a week? Oh, what a hell! But people have gigantic lives. Their families are there, their houses are there, their professions are there, everything is there. They know the territory.

Personally, I'd much rather have my guru just nicely and subtly organize everything. I don't even have to call Him up and ask Him—everything is just nicely organized. To me that is wonderful, it's so relaxing. All I have to do is recognize when the door opens. He's not going to push me through the door—I have to walk through the door—but all I have to do is just see when the door opens. It's wonderful. That's the great thing about being in a lineage under the graceful Influences of all the masters that go back. Everything gets very nicely set up for you. It's like being on a boat, just floating along.

You get what you need. For example, you have a partner or you don't have a partner. When we're desperate for a partner, we tend to make pretty big mistakes. When we relax and wait for the right person to come along, we tend to have the right person come along. In India, particularly in the country, marriages are still arranged. Often young men and women don't have a choice about who they marry, and the percentage of lifelong successful marriages compared to broken marriages is no different than anywhere in the world. A lot of American young people say, "That's terrible, people should have choice. It's terrible that people have to marry who their mothers and fathers decide on." When you look at the mathematics, the percentage of successful marriages is just about the same as for those people who had a choice, which says to me that human choice is mostly an illusion. The Universe decides a lot more for us than we think the Universe is deciding for us.

In any real training, at some point you are going to want to run away. It may be in the beginning, or six months into it, or maybe ten, twenty or thirty years into it—but at some point you are going to want to run away. You're going to feel that the demand is just more than you can bear. It's a very interesting thing. Our school has been around for thirty years now. Most of us think that the thing that is going to make us want to run away is some kind of big task or some major stress or horrible thing we have to confront—like standing in one posture for three days with every muscle in our body screaming for relief! Not necessarily.

We've been around for thirty years as a school, and there are a number of people who have been with me since the beginning or for twenty years. One of the biggest things that makes us want to run away is our fantasy of boredom. People have been around for twenty-five years and the excitement's gone. What's happening? Nothing is happening. Boredom. More people are tempted to run away because they just want something to grip their excitement, to grab their attention, something they feel is interesting instead of the same practices. You get given the practices, and you do those same practices over and over and over. You're practicing for twenty-five years, and you say, "What's the practice?" It's the same as the practice was on the first day you walked in the door. That can get pretty boring. I've found in my school, and in other schools, that the really big demands aren't problems.

In India when they built Yogi Ramsuratkumar's temple, when they had a big job to do they would start early in the morning and work until the job was done, usually ten or twelve hours a day. There's a big dome on one part of the temple that took fifty-five tons of cement. Because the cement had to be cultured in a certain way so that it wouldn't crumble or crack, they couldn't stop until the job was finished. On the day they put in the cement dome, they started at seven in the morning and worked till midnight, even though the workers had families and kids, and they were hungry, or needing a drink—because a lot of them are alcoholics. They stayed on the job until it was done, with no complaint and no question.

I've noticed in our community that people are there for the big things. People can make amazing sacrifices of time, energy and resources when something big is needed. If somebody is dying or sick and needs someone by their bed, people will be there, when before that person got sick they wouldn't spend fifteen minutes with them. They go and sit by their bedside, and they're open and nurturing. When there is a big demand, people will really come out of themselves to meet the demand, but it's the little things that get us. A lot of people who will make absolutely heroic gestures—who won't sleep for days and will go to the last ounce of their energy to complete a construction project—will not go to meditation in the morning. "I don't want to get up that early." Or, we just can't be bothered to say a nice word to somebody when they need to hear a nice word—it's too much trouble.

It's the little things that build up the force of resistance in our system to the Influence of the Divine. Each little thing by itself means nothing, it's so negligible—it really has no effect on your practice. But a thousand little things build up in a big pile inside, and that has got force. We cannot afford to overlook the details of our lives. We cannot afford to be sloppy. I remember twenty-five years ago when we were looking for an ashram in Arizona, we went to look at a place that was for sale. The woman who owned the place was having guests that evening for dinner. It was ten o'clock in the morning and the entire table was set with a tablecloth, silver, crystal and napkins. At the time I didn't understand. I said, "Geez, that woman has some obsessive compulsive neurosis!" But now I do understand.

In America they grade restaurants by stars; five stars is the highest. At one time we had three, five-star restaurants in Arizona, and one of them happened to be very close to our ashram. These two women had a little café in town, and they closed the café because they really wanted to do fine dinners for people. So they bought a house that became the restaurant, and they were open four nights a week from seven to ten. After a year they gave it up, because they couldn't take the amount of work it required to make dinners four nights out of the week, because they were unwilling to sacrifice the integrity of attention to detail. We ate there twice, and it was fabulous.

You go into a restaurant and have this wonderful dinner and in a couple of hours you're finished, and you have no idea that a group of people took twelve hours of their time just to put that meal together. If you aren't in the restaurant business, or if you don't cook yourself, you have no idea what's required—the detail it requires—to produce a particularly fine meal. It's not like opening a can and slopping the salad dressing on the lettuce.

So, the thing that often gets to us, more than the demand to rigorous practice, is actually a lack of attention to detail, which after twenty-five years becomes, "I'm bored." We think that nothing's working. Where's the excitement? Years ago when the Castenada literature hit America, oh my God, people were so excited! "We've had meditation and Buddhism and yoga, but now, *this* is interesting and exciting, especially in Arizona! Oh boy, we can go out in the desert and we can find our own nagual. Who needs Don Juan? Then we can become a student, and it's so exciting . . ."

So, we have to open the doors of ego. Once those doors are open and the Divine gets in, we can't close them as tight as they were closed before. Think very carefully about it before you open the doors of ego. In the Gurdjieff system they say if you are not going to pursue the Path to its end, then don't start. That's because sooner or later you're going to want to run away, and it's going to be a very unpleasant feeling that can make *you* really scary.

ॐ

Darshan

I'm not Yogi Ramsuratkumar. I might be someday, or I might never be. But *if* I were Him, this is what I would say tonight, and this is *all* I would say tonight. A lot of people misunderstand darshan. Not just darshan—a lot of people misunderstand what it is to be in relationship with the guru. Every guru has their own personality, their own style, their own form, their own mood. Some of that is very pleasant and delightful, and some of it is very unpleasant. Sometimes the guru is honey-tongued and always sending arrows of love to his or her devotees, and sometimes the guru is very acid-tongued and is always criticizing and provoking. Sometimes the guru is a little of both.

Sometimes the guru is very clean. There was a guru in India who died a number of years ago, and he never wore the same clothing twice. He always wore white. He would often change two or three or four times a day, so his clothes were always perfectly clean and pressed. He was always bathing. On the other hand, sometimes the guru is very dirty. I wouldn't have called Yogi Ramsuratkumar dirty, but He only bathed once a year or every two years, and He wore the same clothes until His devotees absolutely forced Him to put on something new. Some gurus live on garbage heaps and smear themselves with animal feces or with their own feces. They're really dirty, their hair is matted, and they have flies buzzing around them.

We come to the Path, we find the Path, and maybe we resonate enough with a guru to actually become a student of that particular guru. There are an infinite variety of moods and types and appearances and behaviors in the guru. It's very easy to attribute meaning to the form of the guru. We're thinking beings, so we can attribute meaning to anything; we can make anything appear to be meaningless, or we can make anything appear to be full of profound, deep meaning.

I don't think philosophically. I never find some spiritual point and think about it. In the old days—three, four or five hundred years ago—a lot of spiritual authority was decided by debate. Whoever won the debate was considered to be the highest authority. If someone really had integrity and they lost the debate, they and all of their students would become students of the teacher who won the debate. I imagine more than one person who lost the debate didn't survive the night—in those days it was very easy to get poisoned!

It really annoys me when my students ask me dharma questions, not because I can't answer them, but because it's so boring. I like to listen to other people discuss dharma, it just doesn't interest *me*. Obviously the vast majority of the actual physical time in this seminar has been about considering dharma, so it's not that there isn't a certain time and place in which there is information passed on and there are questions answered. But ultimately all of that is beside the point.

The Universe is a continuous field of energy, and any discreet thing—you or I or this house or a tree or a dog—is a point in that field, distinct and at the same time not separate. Like the many leaves on a tree, each leaf is distinct and yet it's all the tree. That's a very traditional metaphor from India—I didn't think of that! I'm glad I didn't, because it's not a very deep metaphor. They say that Ramakrishna always used to say, "What happens if you take a salt doll and throw it in the ocean? Where is the doll?" The doll dissolves, and what you have is the ocean—yet the doll is a part of the ocean. How about a contemporary metaphor? In America you throw a candy bar in the ocean, and it doesn't dissolve for fifteen or twenty years, because there are a lot of chemicals in those things!

None of your projections on the guru are the point, as optimistic, positive, full of love, devotion, discrimination, power and authority or positivity as your projections may be. No projection or ingredient of mind is the point. The guru—not the guru's physical body, but the *guru*—is a tangent point between the world of illusion and the world of clarity. There is another world that is not separate from this world, and at the same time, it is distinct. We could say it's the world of spirit, or the world of pure being, or the world of consciousness. The guru represents the doorway or the gateway to that world.

The point is that darshan means "sighting" or "to see." In Swami Prajnanpad's teaching the word "see" was used with a very exact connotation. It didn't just mean to look at something with your eyes; it had a very specific meaning. The first year that I was visiting and teaching at Font d'Isiere, Arnaud was very polite to me. He just let me talk and never said anything. A few years later, the first year I taught at his new ashram, Hauteville, he made a small correction: I was using the word "see" the way we use it in America, not the way Swami Prajnanpad used it. Arnaud felt that might be a little confusing to people in the room, so he explained it to me, and unlike most people who call themselves gurus, I wasn't offended at all when he gave me input.

It's interesting that the word "see," the way Swami Prajnanpad used it, and "darshan" may have a very similar connotation. The formality of the prasad ritual—where we offer a gift, bow and receive a gift in return—never bothered me personally. When I was in India I always felt that this was the opportunity to bow at the feet of a genuine teacher, and I had a number of opportunities with different teachers. It was really the highlight of the trip—beyond the amazing temples, swimming in the Ganges, the food, the people, the music, the noise and the lights and everything that India is! But undoubtedly most people would look at our darshan, see you all nicely dressed and bowing at the feet of this American guy, and probably be pretty upset. They'd probably be upset even if I was Japanese, Tibetan or Indian! That would be bad enough, but American?

People are always thinking in the domain of illusion, not in the domain of consciousness. The way the ordinary person sees the formality of this relationship is: "You're giving your power away to somebody; you're a person, you're intelligent, you're independent, you should never give your power to another human being." They completely misunderstand that process and what it is.

Transference doesn't just happen with gurus, it happens with any authority figure. Carl Jung, who was a very famous therapist in the early days of therapy, worked extensively with the phenomena of transference. The majority of the American public—since we did re-elect George Bush—transfers on George Bush as the person who can protect them and keep them safe. Obviously the Republicans play on that fear in order to cultivate and develop and control power and authority. We project all kinds of emotions on all kinds of authority figures.

One of the places I used to like to visit in Paris was the tomb of Jim Morrison in Père Lachaise. The French government didn't want his body there, so they dug him up and sent him back to America. They felt that the kind of attention that Jim

Morrison's tomb was getting was disrespectful and inelegant to all the other great people buried in the cemetery. His tomb was treated as a shrine, as if he was a saint. There was always a crowd of people—mostly in their teens and twenties—praying and meditating around the grave with candles. Often they were smoking some form of hallucinatory herb or drinking heavily, which was one of Jim Morrison's favorite indulgences. All of this is transference. People saw Jim Morrison as their personal savior, someone who could lead them, dancing and singing, to freedom: sexual freedom, consciousness freedom, drug freedom . . . freedom.

It's not uncommon in America that some great sports figure will be accused of rape. It happened recently to Kobe Bryant, the great basketball star, and it also happened to the boxing champion, Mike Tyson. Sports figures have both tremendous support and public antagonism, depending upon which form of transference we have towards that person. Carl Jung understood that this is a phenomenon that happens; it's absurd to wish it wouldn't happen or to tell people to stop it, because people are going to do what they're going to do. Understanding the phenomena, he would work with people so that slowly, over time, they would come to recognize their own transference and take responsibility for it. Then it became possible for the relationship to be what it actually was.

Transference obviously goes on in the spiritual field, and our transference is not the point. We are missing the point if, even unconsciously, we view the guru/disciple relationship and the guru function dualistically, or if we believe that we are born, live and die as separate beings—as if birth, life and death had any meaning at all, except as a part of the natural continuum of the ongoing process of the Universe.

Obviously it is perfectly natural for every human being on the face of the Earth to want health and happiness and safety for their loved ones. It is natural to want to enjoy life and create beauty in some way—to be surrounded by beauty. Some people think that what's ugly is actually beautiful, so any artist, no matter what you do, can be successful! That's the good news if you are an artist; there's somebody who will buy anything! If you are in fact a good artist, that doesn't mean the people who buy your art have any idea at all that you are any better than the worst artist in the world. It's just that they find your things beautiful.

So, we often have an unconscious projection that if the guru is a real guru, the guru is *supposed to* bring us health, happiness and sanctuary for our families and all the things that we wish for very naturally. When we study the stories of spiritual teachers and spiritual communities, we see that what tends to get the most press are the stories in which somebody goes to the guru because their life is a disaster. They surrender to the guru, and all of a sudden they have health, happiness, wealth, professional success and sanctuary for their family. They have everything they always wished and wanted and hoped for! We're led to believe that the function of the guru is to provide for all of us.

It is true that association with the guru does tend to create a circumstance in our lives in which many long-term and immediate problems are instantaneously solved in a miraculous way. People call me up and say, "I've got this emergency . . . I'm rushing my mother or father to the hospital, and I just want you to know." I say, "Great," and hang the phone up. A week later they call back and say, "You know, just the minute I hung the phone up after talking to you, everything seemed to get better. We went to the hospital, and it was a false alarm. My mother is perfectly fine and there's no problem."

When Westerners went to Yogi Ramsuratkumar, they were particularly insensitive to His wishes when His wishes disagreed with their own way of doing things. For instance, I always kept my eyes open in darshan, because darshan is seeing. Okay, yes, we can see with the inner essence of our always-conscious, eternal, stainless, pure being and all that. I always kept my *eyes* open, and when He looked at me I looked at Him—not longer than was appropriate, but long enough. A lot of people didn't do that, because they felt they had to have their eyes closed to actually absorb what He was transmitting. Or they felt, "He's so great and I'm so little and I'm not worthy to meet His gaze," and so they would look down if He looked at them. That really used to annoy Him! I couldn't close my eyes when I was with Him because I'd either fall asleep or go off somewhere—you know, get high.

In either case, I couldn't be responsive to His needs if my eyes were closed. When He was giving me responsibility or work to do, it was obvious that I had to be alert and responsive. It was obvious that if He wanted something, I had to be able to move quickly. Even if there were a thousand people in the room and I was one of them, I would keep my attention *riveted* on Him, because sometimes He would just look through the room and call one of His attendants and point to somebody. He'd somehow fix on one person in the crowd, and He'd want to know something about that person—who they were, where they came from, or what they were doing there. If that person was ignoring Him or asleep or chatting or eating or drunk or whatever, then he or she was not in a state that was responsive to Yogi Ramsuratkumar's communication.

I'd seen people in His darshan who He had asked to give a talk—or perform or sing or something—close their eyes. When He had had enough of them, He would try to get their attention without making noise, but they would be there with their eyes closed, lost in some bliss-world, completely unresponsive to the person they assumed they were serving or obeying! Like all things, there is a time to close your eyes and a time to keep them open.

Darshan is seeing, and the obvious question is: seeing what? The whole point of darshan is that there is no "what," because what it is that we're seeing is not an object. It's not definable; it's not something that we can turn into a concrete definition. The point is that when we have a moment of darshan, we are pulled out of ourselves—not pulled out of who we are as we are, but pulled out of our dualistic, constantly separating, separating, separating minds. That's it! That's the point.

Does that ever happen when somebody looks at a sunset, or is playing with their child or their dog, or is in the kitchen cooking and becomes lost in the task? Sure! But the viability of the sunset or your kitchen or your dog, or your even child (although your child might be at the top of the list of possibility) guiding you along the Path in a way that optimizes your life is unlikely.

It's not like you need the guru because it's impossible to see clearly without the guru; you need the guru because the guru is the tangent point between the created and uncreated. The guru may also be friend, guide, confidant, sage, the voice of experience, but the *point* of the guru is to see Reality, as it is, here and now. Over time, the point is to be able to adhere and abide in that seeing, in which case the guru is not who we thought he or she was. There are still the human qualities of friendship and honor and respect and gratitude, but all of the projections, expectations and illusions—all of the confusion—is what gets taken out of the relationship with the guru.

When I come to Mexico or Europe, where some people see me only once a year, people will often ask, "Is there something we can *do*? Is there a task we can do? Is there some work we can do for you?" I love to give people tasks, but really the success of the task pivots around the fact that the guru is already always with us anyway, not that we need the task to remind us of the guru. After being in Europe for a few months, when I come back to America my students sometimes say, "It was almost better while you were gone!" That's because they don't have the mercurial ways that I behave to distract them from their one-pointed attention on darshan.

I sweep back into America with bags full of little stuff that I bought in Europe and everybody says, "Oh, the Sacred Bazaar is going to be set up again—we'll be spending more money. I'm going to want all that beautiful stuff and not be able to afford it, and Lee is going to be more confusing and paradoxical and enigmatic then ever." When I'm not there, then the good students will find me in their meditation and in their practice, and I'll be solid and steady, essential, always the same. Then I show back up with my personality and everything else, and there is distraction and fascination and seduction and everything else—like who gets invited to the dinner parties and who doesn't. It's endless.

When we have no question if the guru is with us—when we are secure in the presence of the guru, even if we see the guru only once or twice a year—then specific tasks have a different utility and a different effect. I want to give my students tasks, but let me be blunt: I'm a businessman. Everything revolves around *profit;* I want every task to be profitable. When the fact of physical distance and physical separation does not weaken our commitment, our attention, our practice, then a task can be profitable.

We have a publishing company, and maybe fifteen of my students have written books. Very few of those books are profitable for those people in terms of money. If an author makes five hundred or a thousand dollars a year from a book they've written, that can't even buy a good meal for ten people in a decent restaurant in America, so it's meaningless. But it doesn't *cost* them anything to write the book. Your time is not worth *anything*, unless you are using it productively towards the Work.

There is a big difference between physical resources and time and energy. There is an endless amount of time, and you should use it well; there is also an endless amount of energy, and you should use it well. There are not an endless amount of physical resources. Different principles apply to the use of time and energy and money or other physical resources, like your house. I want to see the people who are asking me for tasks learn the lesson of right use of resources. For example, if someone is willing to devote so much time and energy to their task that their children suffer, I don't want to give that person a task. If carrying out a task creates suffering, then it's not profitable to me, no matter what the physical task itself produces. Some gurus couldn't care less: "I don't care about your family. This is the Work. I want you to give everything to the Work, and *you* figure out how to do that." I don't work like that. I agree in principle, but I don't see any conflict between serving your family, being in relationship with a partner, having a certain amount of time and connection with your partner, and serving the Work directly.

So, everybody already has a task. Here's your work: make the guru so abiding and constant in your life that there is no question of distance. Yes, it's always wonderful to see your teacher as much as you can, but life is life, and we all have responsibilities. The teacher is always busy, and you didn't necessarily get born to live on the teacher's ashram, so here you are in Mexico or Europe or New York City or San Francisco. When your relationship to the teacher abides in the presence of the teacher and in no way hinges on or depends on the *physical* presence of the teacher, then you're ready for another task.

Tasks were often given in the Gurdjieff system to create a certain circumstance in which the person who was given the task could learn something. I generally do not give tasks for that reason, because life itself produces all the circumstances we need to learn whatever we need to learn. We don't need big fancy tasks. We're in relationship, we're full of desires, we have to earn a living—what bigger task do we need? All of that produces every lesson we could possibly need about clarity of vision or darshan. For example, every time we go to a meal—any meal, not just a special meal—most of us have to struggle with something, in one way or another. Like when somebody comes to me and says, "I made this dessert just for you," then I have to eat it whether I want to or not.

I tend to give tasks for things that are specifically needed to create greater possibility for the Work. A couple of my students are partners in a flooring business; they sell flooring materials—tiles and stone and wood and all kinds of things. They employ skilled technical people who actually do the installation, and a good installer will make two thousand dollars or more a week. The installer doesn't have to make any investment in materials because it's just their time and energy involved. Of course, you need to have a strong back to do the installation because it requires a lot of physical work with your body always bending over.

Here's an opportunity for many of my students who have been struggling to earn a living for years: go to work for these guys. It takes a few months to learn the skill, then you make a couple thousand dollars a week. People who are making a couple of hundred dollars a week could be making a couple of thousand a week. Very few people are interested, because we want to prove something to ourselves—that we can start our own business! We can do it ourselves! It's ridiculous. Freeing up people's time and energy to have security and lack of worry about paying the bills would make vast amounts of energy and time available to the ashram—but people won't do it. A couple of people have done it; they're the smart ones.

To do a task successfully, *we* can't get in the way, because if we are in the way we are not going to do the task the way the guru wants us to do the task. If in your mind the task is to remind you of the guru, then you're going to be getting in the way of the task. You're going to be, as we say in English, shooting yourself in the foot. So, this is your work: stabilize your relationship to the guru so that, as much delight as you receive from being in his physical presence, it is not *necessary* for your work, for your clarity of mind, for your devotion, for your commitment. The physical presence of the guru is not *necessary*. Then you're ready for a task.

Having a task is secondary anyway—practical, but secondary. What is primary is the moment of *seeing* and the stabilization of that moment so it becomes a process of seeing instead of a moment of seeing. That's ultimately the function of the guru. The guru will be a friend, a guide, a mentor who will give advice and provide teaching lessons as long as necessary. Why not? But none of those are the point. The point is seeing, truly, what is, as it is, here and now, exactly.

Each of us, in our own way, needs to continue to weigh that definition against how we are holding the guru: the projections, the expectations, the needs, the demands—in short, the transference. Yes, it's true that bringing the guru's attention to some difficulty will often relieve the difficulty. We live in a magical world in which reality is very pliable and malleable. The guru is a magical being, so when you engage the guru's attention, you are initiating a certain kind of magic—not the kind of magic that a witch would create, even if it's positive magic. The guru creates magic in a way that is the natural gift of the Universe to its Creation.

That is the point of darshan. We want to have the indefinable certitude of darshan, the moment of seeing, and the instant after that moment fades away we know, "That was it!" We *know* that was it, and we want to keep measuring that indefinable something against the sum of all things that are definable.

One of the things that really annoys people about me is that I'm always contradicting myself. Every moment is unique to itself, and what I say in the moment applies to that moment, but in the next moment it might not apply. For example, I give someone a recommendation, and four years later they say, "Okay I'm ready now," but it doesn't apply now. It's too late. One of my students had a dream years ago about meeting the person who would be his wife somewhere, and for his own reasons he didn't go there to meet her. Now he's ready to go looking for her, but his potential wife was there years ago—now she's married with a family!

So we weigh and measure the moment of seeing against all of the things that distract us. "Lee is really not as accessible as he used to be." Or, "Things have changed, and I don't like the changes." People are always saying, "Lee is always contradicting himself. How am I supposed to know what to believe and how to function if one day he says this and one day he says something else?" I'll walk in the office one day, and someone will say, "So-and-so is doing this." I'll say, "What!? Who the hell told them to do that?!" And they'll say, "You did," and I say, "I must have been in a trance! How could I ever have said that?" I said that because what's perfect in one moment isn't perfect two weeks later.

Once I was yelling at somebody who had been getting instruction and doing the same thing over and over again, ignoring the instruction for fifteen years. I had lost my patience. A new student, who had never seen me get angry, thought that my yelling at this person at the table was really cruel and unnecessary and lacking in compassion. They actually left and never came back. Those kinds of things are going on all the time—we're so *incredibly* naïve.

It's all of those things that distract, confuse and divide us from darshan. You want to continue to measure your knowledge and certitude of darshan against all of the things that are subjective, interpretable and variable. Darshan is objective and absolute. The more you're able to measure the difference between what is objective and what is subjective with some consciousness and attention, the more you'll stop allowing those things to mask darshan and separate you from the guru.

The point of darshan is to see: seeing. Can you have darshan in your heart? Of course you can! Obviously. All of that is true, and we also distinguish darshan with a certain formality for a very particular reason. The formality of our particular protocol of darshan is a way to distinguish darshan over and against the ongoing flow of teachings that happen all the time—the open-hearted river of blessings, the ocean of blessings that's always available.

ॐ